COACHING MODERN SOCCER **ATTACK**

COACHING MODERN SOCCER
ATTACK
ERIC G. BATTY

faber and faber

LONDON · BOSTON

First published in 1980
by Faber and Faber Limited
3 Queen Square London WC1N 3AU
Reprinted in 1986
Printed in Great Britain by
Redwood Burn Limited
Trowbridge, Wiltshire
All rights reserved

© *Eric G. Batty 1980*

British Library Cataloguing in Publication Data

Batty, Eric
  Coaching modern soccer – attack.
  1. Soccer – Coaching
  2. Soccer – Offence
  I. Title
  796.33'423'07   GV943.8

ISBN 0–571–09840–1
ISBN 0 571 11605 1 Pbk

This book is dedicated to my son, Alan Richard, in the hope that he derives as much pleasure from playing football as I did in my younger days, and as I have done as a coach. It is also dedicated to the millions of youngsters the world over who dream of playing at Wembley or Maracana, in the hope that through hard work and good coaching they may achieve their ambitions.

Contents

Acknowledgements

It would be churlish of me not to offer my grateful thanks for all the help given to me over many years by Mr Ron Greenwood. Whenever I dreamed up a new idea I would go to him for confirmation that what I proposed was right. He never actually sat down and said 'Look, this is what the game is about', but, unique amongst English coaches, he was always willing to listen and perhaps offer me a little twist, some slight variation on my suggestion that provoked me to further thought.

I must also thank Dr Geza Kalocsai, now retired in Budapest. He was one of the coaches of the great Hungarian team of 1953–4 and always made me most welcome on my frequent visits to see him coach in several countries, giving me his time and the benefit of his knowledge.

Introduction

Soccer is a simple game, and the secret of good football is to do the simple things well. The diagrams in this book are similar to those in my earlier publication, *Soccer Coaching the Modern Way* (Faber, 1968): at first glance they may seem very complicated, but if you study them carefully it will become clear that they show, in fact, a series of simple actions strung together. There is an essential and well-tried message that I hope runs right through this book: 'Keep it simple, do it early, do it well—and keep on doing it.'

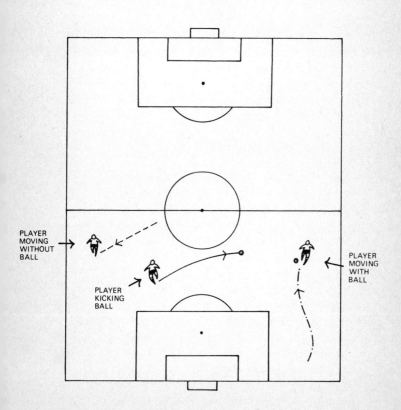

PLAYER
MOVING
WITHOUT
BALL

PLAYER
KICKING
BALL

PLAYER
MOVING
WITH
BALL

Unfortunately, the vast majority of English coaches and managers merely pay lip-service to this old adage; in reality, and particularly when away from home, they have their teams play very defensively with only two strikers (and sometimes only one) upfield all the time. Under pressure, and top-level football is now certainly a business above all else, coaches and managers who could do better feel forced to play for safety, with tragic results for spectators.

Crowds have dwindled right around the world, except in the lesser football countries in Africa and the Far East where the game has only comparatively recently become open to the masses.

At the same time, millions of people across the world watch English Football League matches every week on television. What they see is, very largely, over-aggressive tackling, termed 'getting stuck in'; deliberate foul play, referred to as 'professional fouls', allied to defensive tactics. All this leads me to conclude that if the present trends continue the game will kill itself, and for this I have coined the word 'soccercide'.

This worldwide audience is watching allegedly top-class football that is in reality dull, defensive and dirty; it includes in its numbers amateurs and youngsters, coaches, schoolteachers and youth-club leaders, who are all being steadily indoctrinated in the ways of professional football. Soccercide therefore is not something from the realms of science fiction, even if the day of its coming still lies far in the future.

If television, even unwittingly, encourages players at all levels to do the wrong things, including gamesmanship and unsporting behaviour, it poses a further threat. At some time in the future it is conceivable that the FA Cup Final will be played at an empty Wembley Stadium, watched on television by an audience of thousands of millions across the world. The ruling bodies of the game must recognize the danger and insist that only top-quality, real attacking football is shown on the box, or, even if it costs them money they can ill afford to lose, they must ban the cameras until the game improves, or perhaps allow the screening of only the best two or three teams that try to play real football every week.

During the 1958 World Cup, opposite the Solna Stadion in Stockholm, FIFA put on an exhibition of 'Football Art' at which large prizes were offered to encourage entries with a football theme from all forms of art. I went round the exhibition, and, quizzed at the exit by a lady working there, I told her that football itself was the highest form of art. She replied that she had been told that already more than a thousand times!

There are still plenty of us left who believe that the game should be played the right way but the vast majority have given up watching in desperation. I have the opportunity to try in a small way to do something to help, but in reality football is all things to all men. To the three- and four-year-olds playing in the garden with their fathers it is fun, to the boys who play in kick-about games it is a pleasure, and to the thousands of today's fans it is fast and exciting. To the hundreds involved in professionalism it is a living and a business. To many pseudo-scientists it is a science. You plug-in at any level, wherever you have the opportunity, but certainly the game itself attracts, giving it universal and international appeal. For myself football has been a life-long passion and become almost a way of life. In life you have to be true to yourself, and I have coached and written about the game the way I believe it should be played.

This is where the coaches come in. For the benefit of those many coaches who are open to new ideas, starting with those running teams of boys under eight years right up to the top of the tree, I have written this book in the hope that they will find something interesting on which to work with their players to help make it a more enjoyable game for players and spectators alike.

Soccer Coaching the Modern Way was written with amateur coaches, youth-club leaders and schoolteachers in mind, but in fact it succeeded beyond my wildest hopes and reached a far wider market. After publication, and for some years afterwards, I received letters from national team coaches in Africa, and from coaches in Australia and North America, all telling me they had adopted the coaching method outlined, and describing their successes. I even had a request for a copy from the manager of South Korea. At a higher level, I visited a First Division club in the north of England one day, intending to interview their goalkeeper, but went early to watch the training. To my astonishment, I found the players being coached in one of the combinations in my book, right down to the last detail. Another encouraging feedback came to me from Mr John Lyall, the manager of West Ham. After taking his team on tour in Canada, he told me he had been asked by the Canadian national team coach, 'Do you know Eric Batty?' Apparently he too had worked to the methods described in my book. Finally, *Soccer Coaching the Modern Way* was translated and published in five foreign countries. This included the Soviet Union and Italy, where the FA bought the Italian rights to incorporate the ideas in the official FA coaching handbook. Thus the book succeeded far beyond my original intentions and if *Coaching Modern Soccer— Attack* reaches an equally wide audience, my purpose will have been achieved.

I · *Shooting practices*

Shooting practice must never be neglected. Although modern soccer is more than ever a team game, even packed defences can be penetrated by shots from outside the penalty area, simply because a packed defence obscures the goalkeeper's view, and shots are often deflected by defenders into their own goal.

The development of constructive and intelligent approach play was the theme of *Soccer Coaching the Modern Way*, and though this is vitally important it must never be forgotten that the ultimate objective in the game is to score goals. It follows that shooting practice must always occupy a prominent place in any training programme. The observant reader of my earlier book will have noted that every *combination* or practice always ended with a shot at goal. However this point may not have been emphasized enough. Recognizing this now, it must be clearly stated that the underlying objective in every coaching session should be to score goals, just as it is in match play. It remains true of course that the development of constructive football is essential, but this goes hand in hand with the overall aim of scoring goals. Without the final touch—the shot or header at goal—good football alone, however high the quality, can never bring success in terms of results. Playing good football gives the players and their coach a great deal of satisfaction, but only through scoring goals can all the hard work involved in training and coaching be crowned with the reward it deserves in terms of winning trophies.

This point is brought out and emphasized right at the start of this book because there is a danger that, unwittingly, coaches may give too much attention to the midfield build-up and the creation of shooting positions and neglect the most important thing of all—getting the ball in the net. This may be particularly true when, through good coaching, the team has reached a reasonable level of competence in combined play. An observant coach, however, should recognize this when watching his team in match play. If in training he has begun to over-emphasize the importance of combined play, it will begin to be reflected in competitive games. For example, players in possession of the ball close to the enemy goal will continue to look for colleagues to whom they can give a telling pass when in fact they have already reached a shooting position. Recognizing that players are creatures of habit, there is a constant danger that while the coach is trying to improve the standard of team play, the individual player may begin to lose—or fail to acquire—the habit of shooting.

At the start of every training session it will be a good idea to give everyone a few minutes' shooting practice while the players are warming up. In its simplest form, this practice can be set up by having two or three players, with all the available balls, positioned near one of the corner flags. The goalkeepers take it in turns—two or three minutes each—to face the shooting, and the remaining (shooting) players should be assembled some 30 yards from goal. Making sure that not more than one ball is served at a time, the coach then nominates the shooting players in turn to hit the coming ball. From the region of the corner flag the ball should be played in firmly so that shots can be hit at goal from around 20 yards' range. In this way the shooting players will be forced to go forward *to meet the ball*, and the coach should insist that whenever possible shots should be hit first time. The type of pass played in by the servers will determine what kind of shot is called for, and the coach should therefore ensure that the ball is first played in along the ground and later chipped and lobbed in by drop-kicking the ball out of the hands. The angle from which the ball is played in should also be changed frequently. Thus the shooting players will be forced to make every conceivable kind of shot from the straightforward drive to volleys and half-volleys; as progress is made the ball may even be chipped and flighted over the goalkeeper's head to drop behind him.

From an organizational point of view, several points should be noted. First, the shooting players should be made responsible for retrieving the balls they hit and returning them to the servers' corner—though the spare goalkeeper(s) may help to do this if more than one is available. Second, it will be obvious that the players serving the ball from the corner require shooting practice too, and they should be changed at frequent intervals. Finally, halfway through the time allotted for this practice it should be switched to the other corner flag so that the players can practise shooting first time when the ball comes to them from both the right and the left. It will also ensure, if the ball is played in both accurately and hard enough, that the shooting is done with either foot. On this last point, some players will try to adjust their approach to the ball so that they can shoot with their favoured (best) foot. The coach should watch for this and insist that they try to shoot first time with the appropriate foot, usually the foot that is closest to the ball, i.e. a ball played in from the right should be struck with the right foot, and vice versa.

Developing this practice a little further, the players serving the ball for shooting can be positioned some 20 yards from the corner flag, right beside the touch-line. From there they can dribble the ball forward under close control and then, on reaching the goal line, cross the ball—pulling it back to drop it on or about the edge of the penalty area. Again the players serving the ball should be changed frequently and the crosses should be made first from one flank, then the other.

Two other points should be carefully noted:

1. The shooting players should not be allowed to drift forward too early. The coach must ensure that they time their approach to the ball so that they meet it while moving at speed and shoot first time. Here it may be necessary to make the starting position of the shooting players further back—around 50 yards from goal. Players will still tend to move forward too early, and as a result they will reach the shooting position too soon. In matches this would mean that they would be seen and marked, so it is therefore vital that the coach restrains them, if necessary by not nominating the player to shoot until very late.

2. The player crossing the ball will not be able to pull the ball back to the edge of the penalty area if he tries to do so while running at top speed. Before crossing the ball, the player must momentarily slow down in order to adjust his balance for a quick change of direction. He must also see that the ball is positioned closest to his 'inside' foot, i.e. the left foot on the right wing, and vice versa. He should then be able to swing his right foot (on the right flank) and get it *round* the ball and pull it back hard and high.

Taking this practice another step we can introduce a third man (see Fig. 1a). The server A dribbles the ball forward at speed, pausing to 'set himself' for the skill involved in crossing the ball and, pulling it back, aims his cross for the third man, player B. Now B goes to meet the ball and first time—with head, foot, chest or thigh as appropriate—plays the ball into the path of C who shoots first time.

Two more points should be stressed here:

1. The cross from A must be a high one, otherwise, in match play, it will be too easily intercepted and cleared.

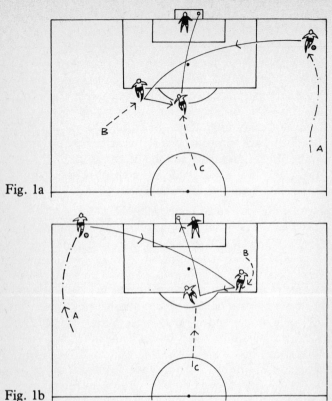

Fig. 1a

Fig. 1b

2. The shooting by C should be performed by the left foot—the one
   closest to the ball.

In Fig. 1b the crosses now come from the left, and the shooting foot is
the right one. Again it must be emphasized that the shooting players
must not begin their approach too early and they should be encouraged to try and shoot first time with the appropriate foot, no matter
how the ball comes to them—on the ground, in the air, or on the
half-volley. Perfect timing of the approach run—and a good lay off
from B—will result in the shot being delivered first time while the
player is moving at or near top-speed. The key factor to watch for,
however, is the quality of the ball from B to C.

   Once more, the players should be changed around at frequent
intervals with everyone except the goalkeepers having a stint at A, B
and C. While it is important that each player should be able to perform

any skill as required and must therefore practise them all, special attention should be paid to the team's central strikers, giving them as much time as possible in the role of player B. In match play they will most often find themselves in situations where they can set up shooting chances for colleagues. But it must also be borne in mind that the purpose of this practice is to improve the shooting ability of the other players, and it is therefore of paramount importance that player B be adept at laying off well-placed balls first time. If player B is unable to perform the skills required then obviously the other players will not receive the kind of balls that will enable them to shoot first time, and if necessary the coach might be advised, temporarily, to take this role himself.

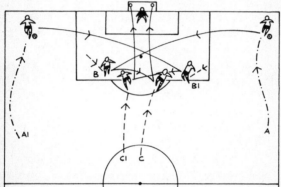

Fig. 1c

If the central strikers in particular are not good at laying off good balls with head, chest, thigh or foot, they should receive special attention from the coach—but at another time. This can be done at an extra training session when the other players are taking part in a conditioned small-side game, or even by remaining behind after the other players have finished training. The participation of other players will be needed to help the central strikers improve their laying-off skill—one to cross the ball, one to shoot, and a goalkeeper. If the reserve team trains at the same time, however, these roles can be filled in turn by players with a central-striker role in matches. Fig. 1c describes a suitable practice, for here we have two sets of players—one group working from the right and the other from the left. A starts the practice with a run and high cross for B who sets the ball up for C to shoot. Then while A, B and C re-position themselves, players A1, B1 and C1 are called upon to go through the same practice from the other flank. The process is then repeated continuously.

It may well be that some of the individual players are good at laying off balls with their head and foot, but not very good when using their chest or thighs. The coach should therefore note such individual weaknesses and instruct players to concentrate on the skills they are lacking, which may well differ from one player to another. The essential of course is that through practice they should improve. Again it may be advisable, especially in the early stages, if the coach himself performs the role of B and asks an assistant coach to be B1. This is the best solution if any of the central strikers are especially poor at laying the ball off with a particular part of their anatomy, on which the coach can then concentrate. In such circumstances the shooting players will probably receive such poor service that they will be unable to shoot at all and will become bored very quickly. This is something that the coach should always be aware of and seek to prevent.

It has already been stressed that whenever technically and physically possible, shots should be made first time. However, only the outstanding *natural* goalscorer is born with the instinctive desire to do so. On this point, though with certain reservations, practical people like myself will agree with the theoreticians that 'players are born, not made'. Yet, despite the general truth of this statement, with regard to first-time shots, it remains a fact that with sufficient practice of the right kind, many other players can develop what eventually becomes an habitual response.

Perhaps this is the point to discuss why it is preferable to shoot first time. As we shall see later, in this respect shooting is no different from the execution of any other football skill or technique. Whatever the circumstances and regardless of what the player receiving a pass may decide to do, it is always best if he does it quickly, i.e. first time whenever possible. The old adage with regard to general principles of play is as true today as it ever was: 'keep it simple, *do it early*, do it well'. In the simplest possible terms this is why first-time shooting is far better than fiddling with the ball to 'tee' it up before shooting. But to go deeper into the question, there are many valid reasons why players should be encouraged (and coached) to shoot *early*.

Shots and shooting positions, like everything else in football as in life, are relative; in this sense, relative to the skill of the player concerned. For example—with the opposing goalkeeper well off his line, a shot from 40 yards might be 'on', but only if the player with the ball is capable of hitting the ball 40 yards. Similarly, a player receiving the ball in front of goal and only 6 yards out *should* be in a first-time shooting position. He should score, but if the ball is coming to him in such a way that a left-foot shot is required, then this will be a 'shooting position' only if he can use his left foot first time.

Having made this clear, we can now say again that if a player is going to shoot, he should do it early. The earliest possible shot is one made first time, hence the emphasis. There are good practical reasons why first-time shooting is desirable.

Any kind of shot, executed quickly, always carries the advantage of surprise: when shooting at goal, obviously the less time the enemy goalkeeper is given, the better. If the ball is played in to a shooting position from one of the flanks (wings), then he will previously have positioned himself to cover the shot aimed at the near post and will also be nicely placed to deal with a high cross if that should be the outcome. Now, as the ball is on its way into what we may call the shooting zone, the goalkeeper has to re-position himself to face the new threat. Clearly, the more time he is given the better it will suit him—and vice versa. Other defenders will attempt to re-position themselves too, trying to put themselves between the player receiving the ball and their goal, or perhaps attempting to get behind their goalkeeper to cover his far post. Time is the vital factor. Given time the goalkeeper will be well positioned, narrowing the shooting angle, and nicely balanced to move either way. Meanwhile his co-defenders will get 'tight' on the player receiving the ball to block (with their bodies) the direct shot at goal; others will cover opponents to whom the ball could be passed, and goal-line cover will be provided too. Going to meet the ball and shooting first time denies the defenders the time to do all these things and, with the element of surprise, gives the would-be scorer the greatest possible chance of success.

In match play, all kinds of factors will determine whether a first-time shot is likely to be advantageous but here we are concerned only with *how* to develop the first-time shooting ability of the players, making sure that the coach understands why shots should be made as early as possible. There will be circumstances in which first-time shooting is impractical, inadvisable and even impossible and for this reason I stress once more: '*do it early*', rather than 'shoot first time'.

I have suggested that shooting should be practised just outside the penalty area for the simple reason that players close to goal need less encouragement to shoot. Most players are reluctant to shoot from a longer range, thinking perhaps that it will be almost impossible to score. This is precisely why goals can be had from such distances—if the aim is good and the ball firmly struck—because the defenders (including the goalkeeper) are more likely to be caught off-guard when someone shoots from around 25 yards.

Before the ball has passed into the shooting zone, the defenders, facing a threat from the flank, will have been massing in front of their goal expecting a cross or centre, so that when it is played into the space just outside the penalty area, all the defenders will be flying about to re-position themselves and in so doing may obstruct the view of their goalkeeper. He will also be on the move and his first 'sight' of a well-hit shot may not come until the ball flies past a defending colleague immediately in front of him. Thus the element of surprise is compounded. Attempting to shoot 'through' a crowded penalty area, packed as they often are with defenders, always carries the chance that someone—friend or foe—may get a touch to the ball and deflect it. Even if the goalkeeper has a clear sight of the ball, as the shooting player sets himself to make his shot, defenders can suddenly close his field of vision or even worse, deflect shots out of his reach.

Observation of First Division football as played in England today reveals that a high proportion of goals which stem from shots made at 20 to 25 yards are in fact deflected—with the goalkeeper already on his way and appearing to have the original shot covered. This knowledge should serve to encourage more shots from around this range, through or over crowded penalty areas. Such a development could significantly increase the number of goals being scored.

Finally, a word about shooting practice during the pre-match kick-around while the players are warming up. Even at First Division matches, players can still be seen teeing the ball up before shooting at goal. In these days of tight marking and quick tackling this is totally unrealistic. Stopping the ball, looking at the goal, then pushing the ball forward before stepping up to shoot should, at top level, be a thing of the past. Hitting a moving ball is far more in keeping with the demands of modern soccer, and players who tee the ball up before shooting are revealing their out-dated habits.

At a period in the game when even defenders are going forward to shoot in match play, everyone should always practise—even in the warm-up—realistically. How much better therefore to play the ball to a colleague and immediately sprint into space—looking for a moving ball played back that can be hit powerfully first time.

II · *Modern wing play*

Wingers are back in fashion though the old style of hugging the touch-line is out. The modern winger is above all very mobile and a striker, roaming into the centre looking for goals as well as providing crosses and passes from the flanks.

Wing play has been coming steadily back into fashion since Brazil won the 1970 World Cup with Jairzinho on the right flank. By 1974 most of the successful World Cup teams had wingers, including the finalists: Johnny Rep and Robbie Rensenbrink for Holland, and Jurgen Grabowski and Bernd Holzenbein for West Germany. Significantly too, the highest scorer in the 1974 World Cup was Poland's right winger Grzegorz Lato. On the other flank, Poland fielded Robert Gadocha, a naturally right-footed player at home on the left who, often to be found deep in enemy territory, also dropped back to work in midfield. By the 1975–6 season, Real Madrid (in Spain), Borussia Mönchengladbach (in West Germany), and Manchester United (in England) were all playing successful football with two striking wingers each. Many other clubs and many national teams were by now using a full-time right winger. But really skilled and effective left-footed left wingers always have been, and still are, very hard to find. More managers and coaches would no doubt field two full wingers if they had them, and despite this drawback it is clear that wingers are firmly back in fashion, though not in England.

The new-style winger is a far cry from players like Stanley Matthews and Tom Finney of England, Julinho and Garrincha of Brazil in the fifties, or Budai and Czibor who starred on the wings in the great Hungarian team of 1952–6. In those days the winger positioned himself near the halfway line and waited for a colleague to give him a pass. Then, depending on his style, he would spring into action. Some, like Matthews and Garrincha as well as Julinho, preferred the ball to be delivered to their feet in order to take on and beat the full back. This was very popular with the fans, though equally effective were the more direct wingers who preferred a through pass which they could run on to and demonstrate their speed. The speed merchants, who pushed the ball into the space beyond the opposing full back, ran and then crossed it for others to score, were easier to find than the highly skilled Matthews–Finney–Julinho types, but they all had two things in common: they ploughed the same furrow up and down their flank, and for long periods they were literally out of the game, waiting for the ball to come to them.

In today's all-action game, every member of the team has to be in the game the whole time if only to keep the team compact. So the new-style winger is quite different from his predecessors.

For myself, I would prefer a winger of the Lato type on both flanks if I could find them, and I am convinced that many teams who still play without wingers could do so if their managers and coaches were willing to take what they regard as a risk. Wingers in Lato's mould have the same goalscoring instinct and ambition as centre forwards; not surprisingly, since Lato himself, in common with many other modern wingers like Jairzinho, was a converted centre forward.

If natural wingers prove difficult to find, switching a reserve centre forward to the right wing (assuming he is a right-sided player) might well, after a little coaching, produce surprising results. This may even be possible with the left flank: after all, Jupp Heynckes of Borussia Mönchengladbach spent the second half of his career on the left wing after being developed as a centre forward. In his new role he proved so effective that he won a regular place on the wing for West Germany and scored many vital goals. Ideally, the modern winger should be good with the ball, skilful enough to dribble past the full back when he has to—and quick enough to stay in front of his opponent once he has got away. He should also be able to shoot with either foot and be good in the air.

But this is only scratching the surface of modern wing play. Wingers must do much more if they are to quell the caution of managers and coaches and reappear in large numbers. If that happens, then wingers will be able to help a great deal in restoring the balance between defence and attack, which in recent years has swung in favour of defence and led to a style of play which is uninteresting to watch.

In addition to having speed, skill and finishing-power, the modern winger must be extremely mobile and therefore in the game the whole time. Like all strikers he should also have certain defensive duties, but in my view these should be limited so that he retains maximum stamina to do the necessary running in attack which constant switching of positions demands.

To stay in the game the whole time the modern winger should drop back down his touch-line when his team are defending, looking for a good short ball out of defence or a throw from his goalkeeper should he suddenly gain possession. In general, his defensive duties should be to challenge any opponent in possession within, say, 15 yards of him. He should also be prepared to harry any opponent in possession on his flank who pops up within 20 yards of the halfway line. If he elects to chase such an opponent he should not give up if play goes beyond this zone, for by so doing he may well confound his defensive colleagues.

Should the winger lose the ball in a tackle, or have a pass intended for him intercepted, he should tackle back at once, if not to win the ball then to hustle the enemy into making a bad pass. Above all, perhaps, if the full back marking him moves upfield to join his forward colleagues, the winger should fall back with him to mark him. He can then hope to intercept any pass intended for the back, and will also be close enough to tackle quickly if the back should gain possession.

But the real value of a modern winger lies in attack.

If an attack develops on the left flank, then the right winger should move inside to become a right centre forward and score his share of goals with headers and shots from balls that are laid in from the left. If an attack develops up the right, the right winger will put himself in the position of the old-fashioned right winger, in what I call his starting position *from where he plays*. Similarly, the left winger will take up his starting position for an attack which develops up the middle, ready to play as an orthodox left winger, but also ready to sprint inside if it becomes clear that in this attack a left winger is not going to be needed.

Of course there will be times—for example if a midfield player breaks through the middle or if the centre forward has gained possession, creating a one-against-one situation, and is about to try and go through alone to reach a shooting position—when the wingers *must* remain wide, hoping to keep the full backs marking them from moving into a covering position.

If a right winger (every move in the account which follows that refers to the right should be reversed to apply to the left) receives the ball in an orthodox wing position he will seek to develop an attack in three basic ways:

1. He will try to get in an orthodox cross, aiming his pass to meet a colleague running across the face of the enemy goal to the near post (see Fig. 2a) or playing the ball beyond the reach of the goalkeeper to a team-mate taking up position beyond the far post (see Fig. 2b).

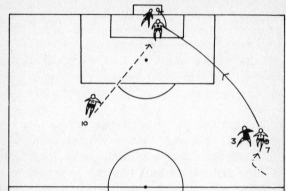

Fig. 2a

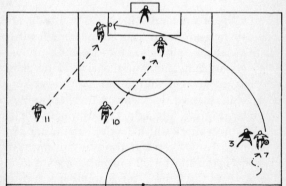

Fig. 2b

2. If there is no one well placed to receive an immediate cross, then the winger, using first his ball skill and then his speed, will try to go past the full back; if the situation is favourable he will then try to cut in towards goal and shoot (see Fig. 3a) or will square the ball to a well-placed colleague after drawing the covering player to him (see Fig. 3b).

3. When the winger receives the ball in a position that is too wide to

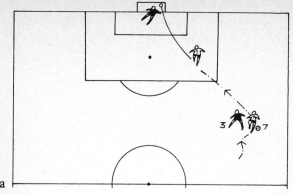

Fig. 3a

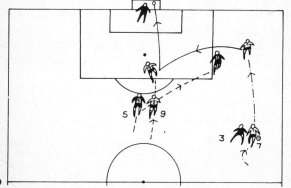

Fig. 3b

allow him to go inside himself, he should use his speed and skill to reach the proximity of the goal line, perhaps laying off a one-two to a team-mate when he meets a covering defender. At any moment he can cross the ball if a colleague appears to be well placed but if he has outstripped all his team-mates he should be aware of everything and everyone around him and pull the ball back, on the ground or in the air according to the circumstances, for a midfield player coming to shoot from the edge of the penalty area or thereabouts (see Fig. 3c).

All three functions used to be performed by the old-fashioned wingers who are regarded as a luxury today. What makes the new breed of wingers different is their mobility, for they should be able to

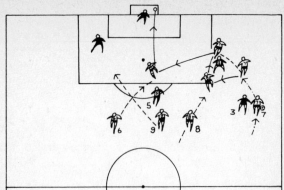

Fig. 3c

pop up at unexpected moments anywhere along the attacking front from outside right to outside left, regardless of their playing number.

In Fig. 4 the ball is being played up to the centre forward, either midfield or slightly left of centre. Being tight marked and under pressure, he cannot shoot himself and plays the ball down into space with his head, chest or foot for right winger 7, sprinting inside, to shoot first time.

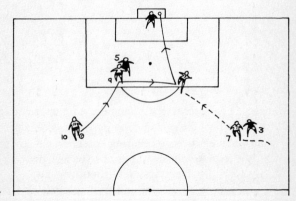

Fig. 4

When the attack develops up the left flank the right winger should, as I have suggested earlier, get inside ready to make a decisive thrust. This could come, for example, when a cross from the left is aimed at the near post. The right winger sprints to meet the ball and attempts to score first time with head or foot (see Fig. 5).

Fig. 5

Alternatively, prior to the cross, centre forward 9 may make the near-post run, and right winger 7 can then move inside looking for a pass not aimed at the near post from which he can head at goal, as in Fig. 6a. With a different cross played almost square across the penalty

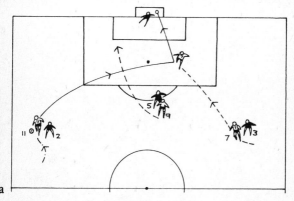

Fig. 6a

area, 9 and 7 can work together: 9 at first goes for the ball but leaves it to confuse defenders while 7, following up, either shoots first time with his left foot or, if the ball arrives at an awkward height, controls it with one touch of his chest or thigh before shooting, again with his left foot (see Fig. 6b).

When the build-up to the enemy goal begins in the centre or on the right flank, the right winger 7 may receive a pass in his withdrawn position. He will not be left unchallenged for long, so he could

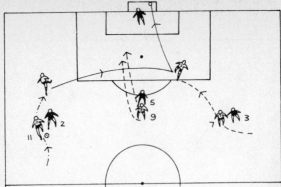

Fig. 6b

perhaps control the ball and turn while centre forward 9 makes a break
down the right flank (see Fig. 7). From his deep position, 7 plays the
ball up the right touch-line for 9 and immediately sprints away
towards the enemy goal, assuming for the moment the role of centre
forward.

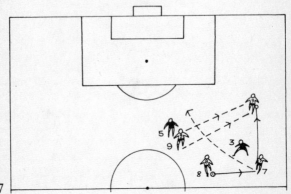

Fig. 7

When coaching all these ploys, it is advisable to begin with
minimum opposition, say a goalkeeper and a centre back to mark
centre forward 9. Later a left winger can be added as required. For
each new practice, the move should be gone through without any
opposition at all except for the goalkeeper, and to begin with should be
done at a gentle trot. When everyone understands his role, the pace
can be accelerated and finally, when everything is going smoothly,

further opposition can be added. It should be noted, however, that the attacking team should in all practices outnumber the defenders by at least one.

Underlining the mobility of the new-style wingers I have already used a key phrase: 'starting position'. With this in mind, players 7, 9 and 11 should position themselves at the kick-off in the orthodox places suggested by the numbers on their backs. But once play has started, all three should seek to pop up anywhere along the entire attacking front and should be equipped with the necessary skills to exploit to the full any shooting opportunities that might occur. In addition to shooting with the wrong foot, i.e. the right winger shooting with the left foot (and vice versa), all three strikers should be able to pass accurately with either foot and to flick the ball on with the outside of either foot. They should also be adept at heading balls coming in from either flank. Almost all right-handed players are better at heading a ball that comes from the left and is headed to the right, vice versa for left-handed players. This is due to overall body co-ordination, though of course a right-handed player *can* head the ball to his left, and will improve still more with practice. Managers and coaches should watch their players closely in practice and in match play for slight weaknesses of this kind: individuals should then be given simple practice in each particular skill as necessary to improve performance.

The ideal situation will be to have three striking players of the centre-forward type. Number 7, whose starting position is out wide on the right flank, should be a naturally right-sided player, and a naturally left-sided player should be at number 11. If they all have the instinct for the goal chance and the urge and ability to shoot or head at goal, if they are all fast and relatively skilful in doing the simple thing quickly and easily, they will be able to feed off each other and constantly change position.

Two simple ways in which the centre forward and a flank player can combine together are described in Figs. 8a and 8b. Though the right winger is illustrated, both moves apply equally to the left winger who should practise them with the centre forward.

Fig. 8a shows the ball being played in to the centre forward 9 from the left. He controls the ball and turns before sprinting off on an angled run moving slightly to the right. As soon as right winger 7 sees that the centre forward is being brought into action he should move inside, eager to give support if required as a right-sided striker. As 9

sets off on his angled run, right winger 7 runs around behind his back
and once there receives a reverse pass from which he can shoot at goal
first time. Here again the opposition should be minimal at first,
perhaps with only a goalkeeper. After two dummy runs a central

Fig. 8a

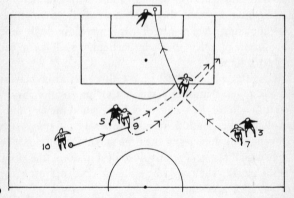

Fig. 8b

defender can be introduced; he should be instructed to lay off 9 at
first, and merely to intervene by positioning himself in such a way that
9 cannot shoot. Once 9 has made his reverse pass to 7, then the
defender can be released to put pressure on the winger to shoot
quickly by intervening and blocking the shot, or tackling if he can.

Another simple practice is described in Fig. 8b. Once more the ball
is fed in to the centre forward 9 from the left. He controls the ball and
turns while right winger 7 sprints inside, angling his run to cross 9's

path. The centre forward should give no prior indication of his intention, but when 7 is a matter of perhaps 2 yards away he should tread on the ball to stop it, leaving it in 7's path. 9 should then sprint away. At first, 7 should be able to shoot first time, but when a central defender is introduced three basic choices are open to him. He can now shoot first time; he can flick the ball on, aiming a return pass for 9 to chase and shoot; or he can control the ball and close in on goal before shooting at it himself. Once players 7 and 9 have become familiar with all three moves the stopper 5 can be released from merely blocking 9's direct path to goal and intervene in any way he can, thus making the practice live, competitive and realistic.

Another simple practice brings in all three strikers, 7, 9 and 11, who assume their starting positions with the wingers out wide on the flanks. The ball is then fed to the centre forward up the middle. After one or two dummy runs against only a goalkeeper to make sure that everyone is familiar with his role, a central defender 5 can once again be introduced, with instructions at first merely to cover 9, not to impede him but simply to block his direct path to goal.

Fig. 9

The practice now proceeds as described in Fig. 9. The centre forward, controlling the ball, turns and makes an angled run slightly to the right. Having allowed 9 to move perhaps ten yards, the defender 5 should now make a determined effort to challenge, and 9, turning away from the enemy and screening the ball from him with his body, should look for support on his right. This should be provided by the right winger 7; 9 lays off the ball to him and then sprints away towards goal. Right winger 7 now crosses the ball first time, aiming his pass for left winger 11 who is sprinting into the penalty area looking for the chance to shoot or head at goal. At this point it may be as well to emphasize to both wingers that whenever the centre forward 9 moves to the right or left (with or without the ball), the winger on the far side should sprint into the centre to become the real, though temporary, centre forward.

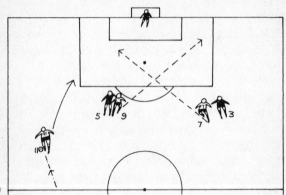

Fig. 10

Fig. 10 shows an attack involving all three strikers in another interchange. This time the ball is fed to the left winger 11, who controls it, turns, looks up, and delivers an accurate cross. As 11 is looking up, centre forward 9 sprints to a position beyond the far post, seeking a chance to head (or volley) at goal from a deeper type cross. At the same time right winger 7, having moved inside as soon as the ball was played out towards 11, sprints across the face of the goal hoping to meet a cross at the near post. If the ball received is not of a kind from which a serious goal attempt can be made, then 7 should be encouraged to flick the ball on towards 9 at the far post; similarly, 9 should be encouraged to nod the ball back across the goal-mouth towards 7. Opposition should again be limited to one central defender who should elect to follow the centre forward or remain in a central covering position. This gives left winger 11 the chance to read a situation and deliver his cross to whichever colleague is best placed with regard to the opposition.

Carrying this theme one step further; should the cross from 11 be aimed at the near post, and either rebound from the woodwork or be half-cleared following a goal attempt by 7 at the near post, it should be 7 who pursues the ball (unless 11 is close) if it rebounds out towards the left-wing corner flag. Should 7 go for the ball then 11 should immediately sprint into the centre while 9 moves from the far post to the near post. Reading across the line of attack now allows us to see the complete mobility of the modern attack for, from right to left, the strikers numbered 11, 9 and 7.

In match play the number 9 will have other duties, being required to drop back looking for balls played up to his feet or, alternatively, making angled runs with and without the ball, both to the left and the right. It follows logically therefore that though the modern attack may be comprised of three players of the centre-forward type, it should be the most intelligent who is asked to wear the number 9 shirt. His role will very often be the key one, and many promising moves may break down if he makes wrong decisions and positions himself badly at the wrong moment, or is difficult to find in the fluid build-up of play.

III · *Second-touch shooting*

Even from 10 yards and less, the height or angle at which the ball arrives may well make it impossible to shoot first time. But second-touch shooting ability can be cultivated. This still satisfies the principle of shooting as early as possible. In addition goals can be scored with the help of cross-winds, by changing the shooting angle at free kicks, by unexpected shots and made from other created situations.

In general terms it is impossible to stress too strongly the importance of first-time shooting, but there are situations in match play when the ball arrives while the player's body is so badly placed that it would require a contortionist to shoot first time. As long as the ball is within playing distance, with practice, anyone can learn to get in a second-touch shot that satisfies the rule of shooting as early as possible.

On first touch, the ball should be flicked with any part of the body permitted by the laws of the game so that it will be in a position from which it can be struck at goal on the volley or half-volley with the second touch. With practice, any playable ball can be turned into a shooting opportunity, and there is still a very good possibility that the goalkeeper will be taken by surprise. Some of the necessary first-touch skills may seem difficult to acquire but my experience has been that good players will quickly pick them up, perhaps after only a few 15-minute practice sessions.

These practices not only enable players to develop the skills required, but also put the idea into their minds that they can quickly turn an apparently hopeless situation to their advantage. Having practised second-touch shooting, a natural goalscorer will quickly incorporate this type of shot into his armoury, and a goal or even a near miss will encourage him to try it more often.

Now let us consider a match situation in which a first-time shot is virtually impossible. The ball in Fig. 11a has been crossed from the right but was cleared by a defender heading the ball out to the edge of the penalty area or by a punch from the goalkeeper. Passing high over the head of the attacking player 8, the ball drops close behind him. If he turns quickly he may be able to reach the ball at the first bounce,

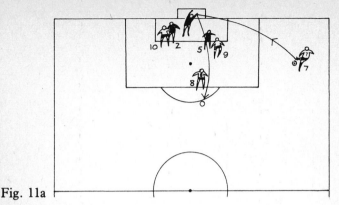

Fig. 11a

but because he is facing away from goal and can only just reach the ball at full stretch with his foot, he cannot possibly shoot first time. With imagination and skill, 8 could flick the ball up and back over his head, adjusting his body and balance as he turns, and with the ball now between him and the goal, shoot with his second touch (see Fig. 11b).

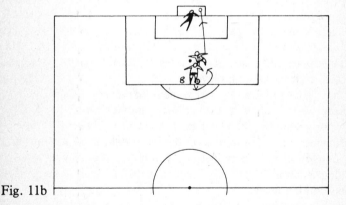

Fig. 11b

A good way to practise this technique is to have a goalkeeper working with three other players. To begin with, these will naturally be three forwards, but eventually all the outfield players should be involved to give them practice. As described in Fig. 11c, the three shooting players position themselves some 15 yards from goal. The goalkeeper starts the practice by throwing the ball over the head of

Fig. 11c

player A who turns and, either before the ball bounces or after one bounce (the quicker the better), flicks the ball back over his head, turning and adjusting his body as he does so. Keeping his eye on the ball all the time, he shoots at goal on the volley. A fifth player can be used to collect balls resulting from wild shots and return them to the goalkeeper who should have several balls at his disposal. He then continues the practice by throwing the ball over the head of player B, and so on in turn. After perhaps five shots each the position of players A, B and C should be changed so that they attempt their shots from different angles and sides. Ten minutes per session will be enough for each set of three shooting players.

It may be as well to stress here something that applies equally to all coaching. It is too much to expect any move or practised skill to produce a goal in the following game. Coaching is essentially a long-term business, and ten minutes a session should be devoted to this type of shooting over a period of weeks. If something positive comes as a result of a new idea after only one session this should be regarded as a bonus, nothing more.

Another situation where a second-touch shot can be suitably used is one in which a high cross reaches a player 15 yards or more from goal at too great a height to be kicked. Headers from 15 yards or more can rarely score because they lack the necessary power to beat a good goalkeeper. Fig. 12a shows player 11 receiving a ball crossed from the right just inside the penalty area. He could head the ball hopefully towards goal, but a much better idea is to control the ball on his chest, if necessary jumping high to do so. Quickly readjusting his body while in the air, he then lands with his left foot on the ground and volleys the ball towards goal with his right foot. Clearly his chest must be withdrawn on contact with the ball so that, by cushioning the impact, it will drop nicely in front of him and he can shoot with real power.

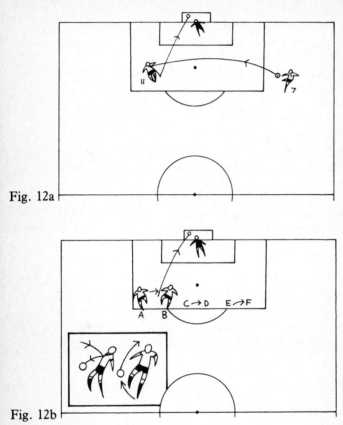

Fig. 12a

Fig. 12b

Fig. 12b describes a practice for six players and a goalkeeper. Bear in mind that with all these second-touch shooting practices, the players, having adjusted their bodies, may at first be unable to reach the ball in time to shoot on the volley. Half-volleys are most likely at first, perhaps even shots after one bounce, but the coach should encourage everyone to hit every ball *as early as possible*: with second-touch shooting this really means on the volley. Once again, the positions of the players should be changed after five shooting attempts

each, and in this practice they should work in pairs facing each other.
Player A throws the ball from around 5 or 6 yards so that B can take it
on his chest, jumping to do so if necessary, and shoot on the turn. The
coach tells each pair when to start so that the goalkeeper is not
subjected to more than one shot at a time. He should call out com-
ments to the players, giving words of encouragement for good
attempts and helpful suggestions about how the skills can be better
executed as well as making criticisms.

With the players facing each other, it will be found that a shooting
player with the goal to his right will be required to deliver a left-footed
volley while players with the goal to their left will have to use their
right foot to shoot at goal. This makes it all the more desirable to
change the position of the pairs of players after, say, fifteen shots each.
As the skill of the players in controlling the ball off their chests
improves, the server can go further and further back, later drop-
kicking the ball out of his hands and, finally, serving a real cross.

When the players have progressed to the point where the server is
crossing the ball in a match-like situation, just as in matches, some of
the crosses will be off target. They will arrive after bouncing or will be
too low to be controlled with the chest. So that the players will know
how to deal with this kind of situation the coach can introduce them to
a third type of second-touch shot—though of course if the ball is
playable first time, the shot should be delivered without a preliminary
touch.

In Fig. 13, the shooting player, facing the server as in the chest-shot
exercise, receives the ball after one bounce. Now, if the ball is within

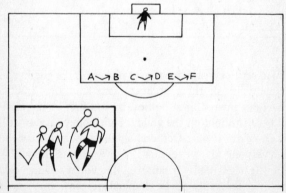

Fig. 13

playing distance but not suitable for first-time shooting, the player can control the ball with his thigh, using the left thigh to control a ball coming in from the right, followed by a right-footed volley—and vice versa for a ball coming from the left. The thigh is used to bring the ball into a position where it can be accurately and powerfully volleyed at goal, and as the ball approaches the shooting player he will have to move, perhaps taking a step back or to one side, or maybe going to meet the ball in order to reach it with his appropriate thigh. It should be emphasized again that the angle of service should be varied, for if the ball comes up to a central striker from an inside-left or inside-right position, the shooting player will have to use his appropriate thigh to turn the ball 'round the corner', quickly adjust his feet, and shoot.

To practise this second-touch shot off the thigh, the players should again work in pairs, as in Fig. 13. The server, at first only 5 or 6 yards away, should throw the ball downwards to give it some 'lift' off the ground from the bounce.

There remains one other second-touch shot that is worth practising. Observation of match play reveals that central strikers very often receive a ball on the ground while they have their backs to goal; an opponent is tight-marking them and there is no one up in close support. While there may well be other solutions, when this situation arises within shooting distance of goal, a really top-class player can, with skill, create a shooting position for himself. Balanced on his left foot, the striker, in Fig. 14, feints to receive the ball with the inside of his right foot and move to his left. This feint should be made a fraction early, to allow himself time to come back and flick the ball up using

Fig. 14

the toe and instep of his right foot to bring it into a position roughly level with his right hip. As his right foot comes to ground he should swivel so that it is pointing towards goal. He can then pivot on his right leg and volley towards goal with his left foot.

To practise this skill the players should again be paired off, as in Fig. 14, with the servers, players A, B and C, positioned (for accuracy at first) only about 10 yards away. The shooting players should be about 4 yards apart, some 18 yards from goal. Player A pushes the ball forward along the ground to player D who throws his feint, comes back to flick the ball up with his right foot, turns, and volleys with his left. Again the serving and shooting players should change places after five shots. To give practice at volleying and flicking up with both the left and right feet, the pairs should be switched round after each player has had fifteen shots at goal.

With all these practices, an extra player to field balls behind the goal, a goalkeeper, and plenty of balls will be necessary. It may also be found that, because of lack of skill, the quality of the service is not what it should be. Nothing can be more frustrating for a player wanting to control the ball with his chest or thigh to find that it comes along the ground, for example. Therefore, if the practice is falling down because the service is poor, the coach should immediately step in, at any stage, and insist that in the interests of accuracy, all balls are served by being thrown rather than kicked.

The result of all this practice, if made a regular part of the training programme, should be a much higher number of shots at the enemy goal and consequently more goals. Some players may experience difficulty at first in controlling the ball with the various first touches to get it into a volleying position, and others may at first be unable to readjust their bodies quickly enough to get in a volley. But given time, encouragement, and patience, in the hands of a good coach the players should begin to produce goals from second-touch shots.

Ajax Amsterdam 1971–3

One of the most notable recent examples of frequent and accurate first-time shooting was provided by Ajax Amsterdam in the period 1971–3. Such shooting power as that which they revealed could only be the result of a great deal of practice, combined with a high degree of confidence and a lot of encouragement from their coach. The Ajax midfield players, and even the back four, were eager to shoot at every opportunity from around 25 yards. Many of their shots were saved by the goalkeeper (in theory a goalkeeper should be able to get to everything hit at him from more than 20 yards), while others hit defenders or went wide, but a very high proportion produced goals.

Shooting like this, with real power and accuracy, can only come after a good deal of practice: shooting is as much a habit as a skill. If players have not acquired the habit in training of shooting first time from a long range, they will not do so in matches. The frequency with which the Ajax players shot from long range during the years mentioned was also a tribute to their confidence. In lesser sides, the players want to pass rather than shoot—passing responsibility, too, with the ball.

A player who shoots as hard as he can every time he can is a player who has confidence. Without this quality, a player will be afraid to shoot from around 25 yards, particularly first time, in case the ball goes hopelessly wide or high over the bar. He is then likely to be derided by the crowd and criticized by his colleagues who, at best, may say that he should have passed to someone better placed, or may accuse him of being 'greedy'—of wanting to score fantastic goals and playing for himself rather than the team. It follows therefore that the coach must adopt a positive attitude and insist that all the players should have a go every time they receive the ball within reasonable shooting range, even up to 30 yards. He should be equally adamant that the shooting player should be complimented by everyone for a good try—whatever the outcome.

Many of the long-range goals scored by Ajax players during these years came from nothing more than a variation of the one-two (double pass on the Continent). Following an all-out assault on the enemy goal perhaps four men would be around the edge of the enemy penalty area when a ball was half-cleared into no-man's-land. Pounced on by an Ajax midfield player or by one of their back-four players going forward, from perhaps 40 to 45 yards from goal the ball would be pushed forward to an attacking player. Two alternative moves are shown in Fig. 15. The front player moves to meet the ball and simply lays it back into space first time. Meanwhile, the man who played the ball up, laid his pass and kept going. Looking for the ball back, he takes the chance to shoot first time from longer than normal range. In Fig. 15, midfield player 8 plays the ball up to 9 and shoots from the ball laid back into his path; alternatively, the back-four player 6 plays the ball

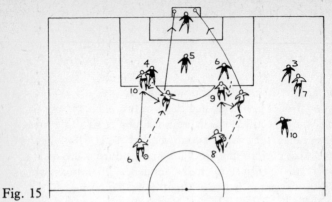

Fig. 15

up to 10 and follows up looking for the ball laid back from which he can shoot.

Many more long-range shots from Ajax at this period were set up by their nominal left winger Piet Keizer. A player of Gadocha's type of game, he attacked up the left flank *from midfield*. Being an exceptionally gifted player, Keizer was able successfully to take on most opponents and then, fairly close to goal, would reduce the speed of the game to walking pace and often even stop it—with the ball at his feet standing motionless. Looking about, Keizer would frequently see a shooting space inside and call a back-four colleague to come forward, looking for a square pass in a long-range shooting position, as described in Fig. 16.

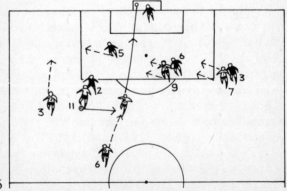

Fig. 16

There are many other situations in which an exceptionally good player can take advantage of special circumstances to get in a long-range scoring attempt. Perhaps the most memorable was Pelé's effort from near the halfway line in the 1970 World Cup game against Czechoslovakia, when Pelé, in possession, spotted the Czech goalkeeper Ivo Viktor well off his line. In the event, the ball bounced just wide of the goal but there is no doubt that Viktor, almost on the edge of his penalty area, had been beaten.

Having watched international football in many countries for more than thirty years I have occasionally seen the exceptionally gifted player take advantage of a slight cross-wind to shoot successfully from around 30 yards. Such an idea never enters the heads of many players who have the skill to curl and bend their shots, but there is no reason why more such attempts should not be made, particularly since, as the case of Viktor v Pelé illustrated, it is the practice of good goalkeepers to come off their line when the ball is in midfield—halfway out to meet a long pass dropped behind the line of defenders. Not all players will have the presence of mind to think of cross-winds during a hectic competitive match, but perhaps the two or three most skilful and intelligent players might benefit from a little practice and encouragement from their coach. All that is needed is a favourable wind, a few minutes' practice, and the aid of a goalkeeper.

As Fig. 17 shows, the coach should have the ball close to the halfway line with the goalkeeper positioned, say, 12 to 15 yards off his line. As the ball gets closer to the goal, the goalkeeper will work his way back. The coach should push the ball forward for player A to run on to.

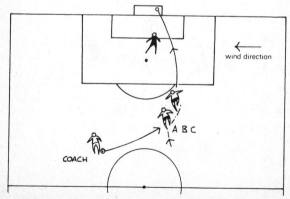

Fig. 17

Looking up to view the passing situation in match play, the midfield player with imagination glances at the goalkeeper, spots him off his line, and feels the cross-wind on his cheek. With a wind blowing from right to left, the midfield player A should aim his shot, curling it with the inside of his right foot, for a mark, say, 3 to 4 yards 'beyond' the goalkeeper's left-hand post, as in Fig. 17. Without any *bend* on the ball and without the cross-wind, the ball would pass, if accurately struck, 3 or 4 yards wide, but if the ball is given slightly more lift than usual, allowing it to hang in the air a bit, the wind will take it and make it swing back, assisting the bend imparted by playing the ball with the inside of the right foot. Players B and C can then make an attempt from the same position, aiming at the goalkeeper's right-hand post if the ball is struck with the inside of the left foot or with the outside of the right foot. Either way, a little curling effect will be imparted to the ball.

The same cross-wind could also be used to help score goals with dead-ball efforts from free kicks close to goal. But defensive walls these days should always extend at least two men beyond covering the near post, making it more difficult to bend the ball round the wall and in. However, it can be tried and the stronger the wind, the greater chance of success. Another ploy which is being increasingly used by good teams when taking free kicks close to the enemy penalty area is to change the angle of the shot by passing the ball square or even pulling the ball slightly back towards their own goal.

A typical free-kick situation is described in Fig. 18: a defensive wall covers the shot at the near post and beyond, all the players in the

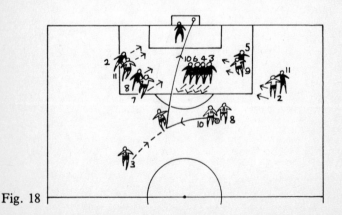

Fig. 18

penalty area are tightly marked, and anyone in a wide position is also covered. If the ball is now pulled back, away from goal, it makes it more difficult to get tight on the man receiving the ball; if he shoots first time the chances are that no one will get close enough to block such a shot. Changing the angle opens up the path 'inside' the wall towards the near post, which is the goalkeeper's weakest spot at the moment the kick is taken. In addition, all the advantages described in Chapter I will apply: friend and foe will be flying about the penalty area reducing the goalkeeper's field of vision, and there is also the possibility that such a shot might get a deflection.

All the practices described in this chapter are aimed at producing more shots on target. Without shooting, a team cannot score, and it follows naturally that with more shots from what are usually considered non-shooting positions, the more the enemy goalkeeper will be tested and, one hopes, the more often he will be beaten. It can never do any harm to shoot, and if shots are tried in the situations described here, the enemy goalkeeper will certainly be kept active.

IV · *Blind-side runs leading to goals*

Blind-side running appears to have become a lost art. Basically, players should try to get away from the area around the ball; then, by changing the direction of the attack, they can make blind-side runs, looking for longer passes. There are also situations where well-coached players can consistently make blind-side runs leading to goal chances.

One of the least discussed techniques in soccer is the art of blind-side running, i.e. passing an opponent on his blind side (behind his back and out of his field of vision) in order to receive a through pass. Though by no means impossible, wingers and centre forwards, being tightly marked, cannot always easily do this nowadays. But midfield and the back-four players can invariably make a blind-side run at almost any given moment.

Perhaps the simplest way of introducing players to this particular art is to show them two or three different versions, which I shall discuss in a moment. This can then be followed by a small-sided game, and when they become proficient at it, a game between two full sides in which it is a condition that goals scored do not count *unless the build-up to goal includes at least one blind-side run.*

In Fig. 19a, right back 2 has just won possession of the ball from his

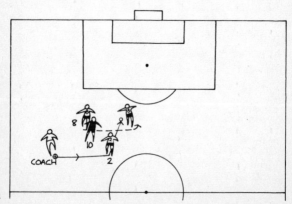

Fig. 19a

winger, either in a tackle or by interception. As he looks up, opponent
10 is close enough to offer a challenge and in any case, wanting to build
a quick counter-attack, the right back will be unwilling to risk having
to dribble. His midfield colleague 8 is well placed to spring across into
space, and if he makes no call for the ball as he goes, the enemy *10* will
probably not know he is there until he turns to follow the flight of the
pass from the right back.

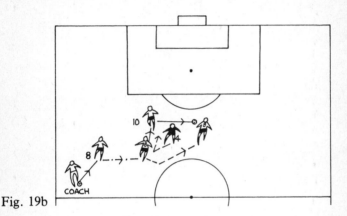

Fig. 19b

For two midfield players a slightly more difficult, though just as
effective blind-side run can be set up as described in Fig. 19b. This
involves players 8 and 10. Inside right 8 has possession of the ball and
is moving upfield, looking to see where he can best lay his pass, when
opponent *4* decides to come across and challenge. Just before opponent *4* reaches a tackling, or even an interception, position, player 8
dispatches the ball to his left for midfield colleague 10, and immediately drifts casually off towards his right. Now 8 watches opponent *4*
closely and as soon as he turns once more to have a go at player 10, who
is now in possession, player 8 sprints forward looking for the through
pass from 10, across the back of the opponent.

A blind-side run involving a midfield player 4 and strikers 9 and 10
or 9 and 11 is described in Fig. 19c. Player 4, in possession, pushes or
chips the ball up, depending on the distance it has to cover, to be
played by the feet of centre forward 9. He then moves into space on his
right, looking for the ball back. Meanwhile, centre forward 9 sprints
to meet the ball, drawing off his marker 5. Because he was aware of
what was coming and has moved first, he beats him to the ball and

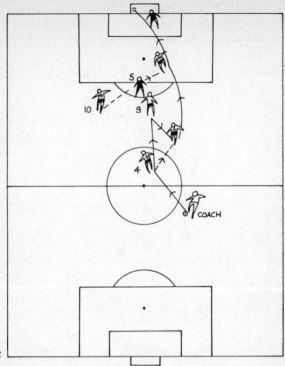

Fig. 19c

plays it back first time to player 4 in his new position. Timing his run nicely, taking into account the distance he has to cover, player 10 now makes his run on the blind-side of stopper 5, looking for a through ball from 4. It should be noted that it is player 10 who dictates where and when the ball from 4 is played, for only a pass from 4 to 10 that is delivered into the right place at the right time and is playable first time will be a good one. In match play, player 10 should try to ensure that his run minimizes the effectiveness of the cover a *libero*, or free back, could give. He could do this, for example, by calling for a 'chip' from 4 to where he is now, and so perhaps draw the *libero* to him and then, by sprinting off across the pitch, catch him running the wrong way. But for the moment ignore the *libero* and allow the players to familiarize themselves with the move as described.

   All these practices should at first be gone through with only the players directly involved. After two or three dummy runs the players should all understand what is required of them, and from then on striking players can be positioned upfield with them so that an attack can be pressed towards goal following the blind-side run. Make sure, when following the practice in Fig. 19c, that player 4 is not too close to centre forward 9; player 10, on the other hand, should not be too far away, at the maximum, say, 10 to 12 yards.

As a general principle of play, players who make blind-side runs from defensive positions or in midfield are producing more attractive, more progressive football than players who merely exchange short passes with unmarked colleagues. This is seen too often, and while exchanging easy balls may look good, it is unproductive and wastes time. Wherever possible, players should be encouraged to make positive passes that will be beneficial in terms of building an attack, and this, of course, must be the primary aim every time the ball is won. Naturally, this does not mean that a player in possession but under pressure can never give off an easy ball, but a defending player who suddenly gains possession should always look and think creatively, trying to set off a quick counter-attack. There are two very good reasons for this:

1. Exchanging unproductive passes not merely wastes time; it gives time to the opposition. Opponents who were attacking and are now out of position have full opportunity to sprint back and take up their covering roles.
2. The quick positive ball which sends play immediately towards the opponent's goal may cut out as many as five or six opponents who will temporarily be unable to interfere with the counter-attack.

Fig. 20 describes how a very good telling pass from left back 3 combined with a blind-side run from midfield player 10 can temporarily cut out no fewer than seven opponents. Such a move gives the team that is counter-attacking a very real advantage if they are able to press home their attack with speed, accurate passing and intelligence. With the enemy attacking in strength, the left back 3 gained possession of the ball either by interception or by a good tackle on his man, the right winger 7. There is space upfield on the left flank and midfield player 10 is making a blind-side run across the backs of opponents 4 and 2. The left back 3 therefore lobs a long high pass away up the left for 10 to collect and mount a quick counter-attack.

It may be argued that teams today do not leave such spaces, that such opportunities do not arise. But I will show in a moment that just

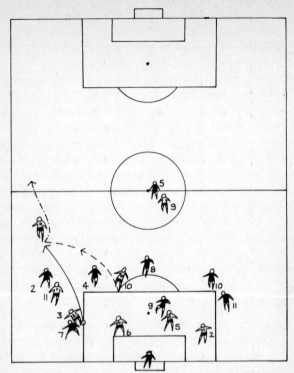

Fig. 20

such a move provided West Germany with their winning goal in the 1974 World Cup final. However, before moving on to this, there is a further point already touched on that requires clarification.

Fig. 20 shows a situation in which a defender suddenly gains the ball and, looking up, sees a colleague running looking for a telling pass—with the result in this case that no fewer than seven opponents are caught out of position. All seven are now temporarily out of the game and will not get back into it unless the counter-attacking team delays its move. But more than that, the players with defensive duties have been disorientated. The quick pass out of defence left *2, 4, 8* and *10* all out of position and to get back to fulfil their defensive duties they must all sprint back in the shortest possible time. Their paths—heading straight for their own goal—will not necessarily coincide with the paths now being taken by the opponents they are supposed to mark. Temporarily almost everyone is free and unmarked, able to use his initiative. The three attacking players caught out of position *have been turned round*. Turning round to assess the new situation, they have lost their sense of orientation and have lost contact, too, with the men they should be marking, who are now free to make runs on their blind sides and confuse them still further.

Because there are still a few top-quality players about, it is possible to see good blind-side runs occasionally. It seems probable, though, that in most cases they pass unnoticed. One spectacular and important goal involving a blind-side run will surely be recalled by all, though not necessarily because of the blind-side run. This was the goal scored by Gerd Müller for West Germany against Holland in the 1974 World Cup final. Franz Beckenbauer began the move from deep in his own half, flighting a long pass across the pitch aimed for right winger Jurgen Grabowski. The pass was dropped in short of the winger (i.e. nearer his own goal than the player) who was therefore forced to drop

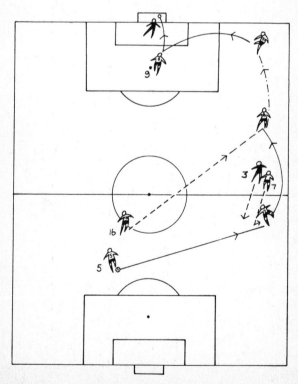

Fig. 21

back to collect the ball. In so doing he drew forward the Dutch player marking him and, quite unnoticed, Rainer Bonhof (16) steamed across on a 50-yard run from left midfield to the right wing, running on the blind side of countless Dutch players who were ball-watching, and also of the Dutch left back. Grabowski played the ball up the right wing, and there was Bonhof, away on his own, able to collect the ball, cut in, and lay on the pass from which Müller scored what proved to be the winning goal. Because few people are fortunate enough to have cine equipment and a film of the match, the move is described in Fig. 21 with Beckenbauer 5, Grabowski 7 and Bonhof 16.

The success of a blind-side run at this level—a straightforward, very elementary move—must bewilder those who claim that the Italian-style defences we see today, complete with a free back, make such simple moves impossible. But the secret of good football is, as it has always been, simplicity. 'Keep it simple, do it early, do it well.'

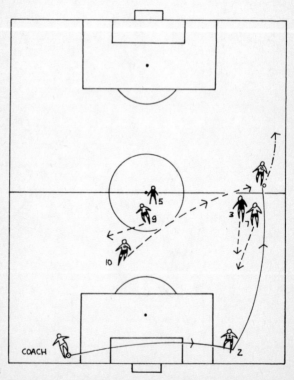

Fig. 22a

There are any number of other practices that will enable the players to get into the habit of making blind-side runs almost naturally; Fig. 22a illustrates one in particular that is a slight variation of the one that Bonhof made to create the 1974 World Cup goal. Cross-field passes, changing the direction of the attack, often create favourable conditions for players to get on the blind side of their immediate opponents. The coach creates one here to start this practice with a pass from the left to right back 2. Before making the pass, the coach had looked up towards the centre forward, calling him by name, and 9 dropped back, looking for a pass to create a diversion and add to the space available for left midfield player 10.

As the right back 2 brings the ball under control, right winger 7 drops back looking for a ball at his feet; at this point in the practice, the coach should insist that the opposing left back 3 goes tight with 7. As 10 makes his run on the blind side of left back 3, right back 2 chips

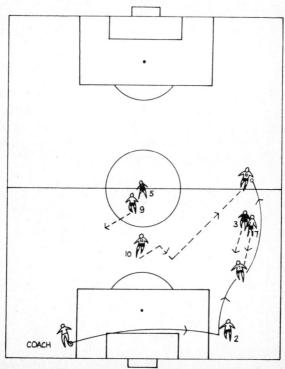

Fig. 22b

a longer pass upfield, dropping the ball nicely in the path of 10. From there, centre forward 9, and 10 on the ball, attempt to break past defender 5 and create a shooting position in any way they like. From their deep position, right winger 7 and right back 2, although temporarily cut out of the game, should also be encouraged by the coach to try and get forward to help.

Fig. 22b shows a variation of this blind-side run by 10, which arises if defending left back 3 should elect not to go tight on right winger 7, preferring to wait and see what develops rather than expose his back. This is in fact what an intelligent left back would begin to do in match play if 2, 7 and 10 succeeded in putting 10 away on his blind side once or twice. Realizing that 7 has not created space for a blind-side run, in this practice, left midfield 10 checks while right back 2 plays the ball up to right winger 7. He controls the ball and turns to run at his opponent 3 with 10 in close support for a one-two if the winger wants him. Now, as left back 3 closes on player 7 who is in possession and coming at him, player 10 might even yet manage to get forward on his blind side to receive a pass from the winger and get away up the right. Whatever happens, the coach, as always, should insist that the attack be pressed to a shot on goal.

The centre forward, and indeed any attacking player, can often get away 'on the blind' in one-against-one duels, but it should be stressed that this is true only of really top-quality players who, working in pairs (one in support), have a very high degree of skill and intelligence. A very simple practice involving two players against one should precede the attempts to get away on the blind and the coach will quickly realize whether his players are good enough or not.

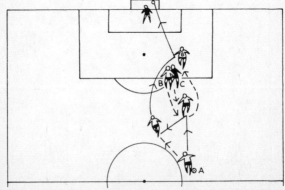

Fig. 23a

In Fig. 23a player A pushes the ball forward for player B to drop back and meet it. Marked by defender C who can in this practice come tight on B or not, just as he pleases, B has two alternatives. If he is first to the ball and C is moving forward at speed *and very tight*, B can touch the ball back to A and be gone, looking for a return pass over the top of C. If C lays off as in Fig. 23b player B can turn on the ball and try to get in a shot at goal while defender C tries to block it.

Fig. 23b

Now, by giving this practice an extra twist, it can be made much more difficult. Defender C is instructed to stay tight on B all the time, strictly man-for-man to the exclusion of all else. Before A makes his pass, B should be told to make a feint to break forward, then to check out and come back looking for the ball short at his feet. Defender C will not be far behind, but will be wary (facing two opponents) and not easily caught. In this practice, described in Fig. 23c, time is not important. What is essential is that players A and B should make the right decision and both come to the same conclusion. Having drawn C tight with a ball played to the feet of B, the latter touches it back and attempts to break away. Has he got away? If so then A should chip the ball over C for B to run on to. But if B has not got away, then A and B should attempt to exchange passes again, trying once more to get B clear of C's attentions.

If C is good, intelligent and quick, it will be extremely difficult for B to get away. If B does get clear momentarily, then he wants the ball dropped in just right for him *at once*. If he does *not* get away, he will check out and look for the ball to be played in short again—to drop

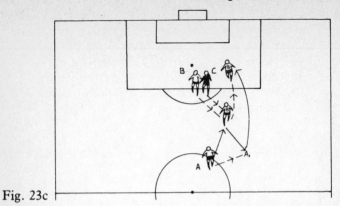

Fig. 23c

back to at his feet. In my experience, A will often misread the situation and chip the ball forward when B is not clear of C. Or, B will get clear momentarily, and either A will not realize it quickly enough or will not have the skill to drop the ball in where it is wanted. Another common mistake is that player B will think he has not got away, or will decide correctly that he has not, while player A thinks B is free and plays the ball forward. This practice, which looks very simple, requires a very, very high degree of ability. Try it on your players, and only if they can make it work should you go on to the practice in Fig. 23d.

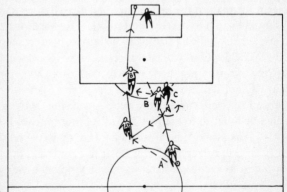

Fig. 23d

This is a slight variation of the previous practice. Player A pushes the ball forward for B to drop back. With C tight on him, he plays the ball off first time and tries to get away. As B makes his break, player C (the defender) may well turn in such a way that for a moment he shows his back to player B, who immediately checks out, sprints across to his left, and takes a good second ball from A to shoot on the turn, first time. I once saw Gerd Müller of FC Bayern München and West Germany do this successfully, but it should again be emphasized that only two players of the very highest class will be able to carry it off successfully. With players of less than really top quality it will probably be a waste of training time—but try it.

In those happy far-off days of WM it was very common to see centre forwards roaming to the wings (making runs across the backs of the full backs on either flank) in search of long passes—and getting the ball. From there they could either cut in towards goal themselves or cross for someone else to go in and make an attempt on goal. Today, however, though central spearheads can still use the flanks and may get momentarily free, there will surely be a defender, trying to tight-mark them, close on their heels.

When central strikers make such runs today, they will, on receiving the ball, require a great deal of skill if they are to turn on the ball before their shadow arrives, and even more skill to take him on and go by him. Again, a good player should be encouraged to try it, but in case the central strikers attempt such a run and get into trouble, it will be a good idea for the coach to set it up in training and, using supporting players, enable the striker (9 in Fig. 24) to get himself clear if he receives a ball up the flank(s) with a tight-marking defender right on his back.

In Fig. 24 the centre forward has made a blind-side run out wide on the right flank and received a ball played up the wing to him. In match play, if he has the time—relative to his skill—he will take the defender 5 on and cut in or else will get in an early cross before 5 can get tight enough. Player 9 does not need any practice to do this, but if he tries to get away free and fails, but receives the ball, good running by some of his colleagues will enable him to get out of trouble if he is in it.

For this practice the coach should instruct the centre back 5 to tight mark his opponent 9 who receives a long pass up the right from the coach. Right winger 7 should be told to try and 'get inside', if only to take the left back 3 away from the supporting players, but also to be ready to get into a scoring position from the cross that follows. Meanwhile right back 2 and right midfield 4 should be instructed to run to take up supporting positions, looking for a first-time ball from 9 if he is in real trouble with defender 5 right on his back. In practice the

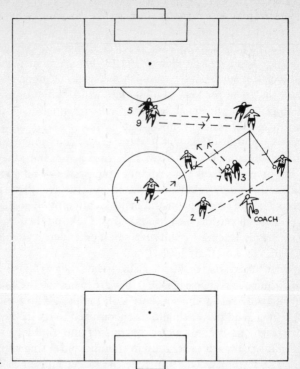

Fig. 24

centre forward should play the ball back to either 2 or 4 who are in a
position to make a through pass if circumstances are favourable, at
worst they should be able to cross the ball.

The approach by players 2 and 4 should be timed to fit in with their
colleague 9, for they must not get too close too early or they will be
forced to play the ball 'blind' if an opponent is chasing them, and the
result could be a common-or-garden 'hopeful' high cross into the
enemy penalty area. If player 9 has time to control the ball before
laying it back, if he has time to turn for example, but knows from
previous experience that he lacks either the skill or pace to beat
defender 5, then the ball back will come fractionally later, and supporting players 2 and 4 should time their approach according to the
circumstances in which 9 finds himself. If he needs support first time,
then 2 and 4 should try to get into good supporting positions to receive
such a pass, but if they get there too soon, they will, as always in such

unfavourable circumstances, have no time to look up and survey the situation in the middle (in the time that the ball takes to get within playing distance) and make an intelligent decision. In other words, they will have no space to play in. Incidentally, Chapter V deals with crosses from situations such as this.

Around 1974–5, Trevor Brooking of West Ham began to make blind-side runs down the left flank with devastating effect. Many of these runs led directly to goals, but it should be emphasized that Brooking's skill, his ability to feint to cross and turn away while always screening the ball, enabled him to get away with things that lesser players could not have done in that relatively confined space near the left-wing corner flag. Because attacking midfield players lack the skills of Brooking does not necessarily mean that blind-side runs from midfield should not be tried. The practice described in Fig. 25a

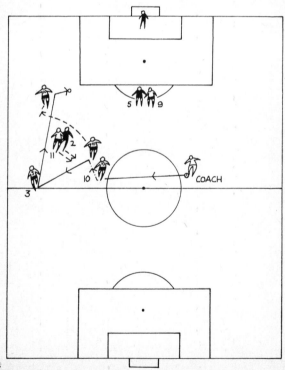

Fig. 25a

will give players the basic idea. The use to which such a run is put, indeed its success, will depend on its timing and the quality of the ball that is laid in for the runner, but this of course is true of all coaching in game situations. I stress this point only because coaches who have seen Brooking achieve miracles may be disappointed that their players can only get in orthodox crosses. Again, the remarks in the next chapter should be helpful and of interest here.

The coach should start the practice with a pass to left midfield 10, as in Fig. 25a, who turns on the ball, takes a few steps with it, and then releases it to his colleague 3 who has moved up in support. Left winger 11, marked by defender 2, can help out by dropping back, looking for the ball played up to his feet; meanwhile 10 makes his diagonal run across the back of defender 2 and receives the ball played up the left touch-line by 3. According to the pace of 3's ball, 10 should get himself 'round' the ball on to the far side as he approaches its path, and

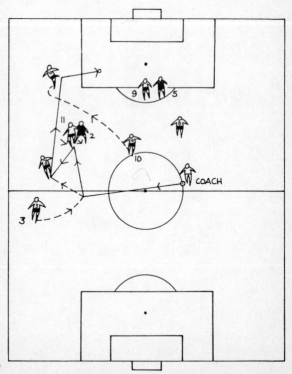

Fig. 25b

should also look right as he makes his run to survey the situation both on his back and in the middle. Assuming that there is no one on his back and no defender coming out who can reach the ball before him, the 10 looks up, makes his decision and, according to what he has seen, makes his cross.

An alternative approach to this basic move is described in Fig. 25b. The coach starts the move with his pass to the left back 3. Left winger 11 drops back to receive a ball nicely dropped in short for him at his feet and, with defender 2 tight on his back, plays the ball back as illustrated for left back 3, who has moved up and gone wider, looking for the return pass. With the ball on its way from 11 to 3, left midfield 10 sets off across the back of 2, again looking for the ball down the line from left back 3. Once more he looks right to see what is happening, and once more he gets himself on to the other side of the ball (if he has time) so that he can cross the ball first time.

In match play it may happen that though the blind-side run from 10 (or any other midfield player) is successful and he receives the ball played up the line from left back 3, an enemy defender on his way out to get tight on him prevents him from crossing the ball. 10's colleagues should automatically take up supporting positions just as they did for the central striker in an earlier practice, so that if he needs a player to lay the ball back to, then 3, 11 or 8 are handily placed. The coach would be well advised to practise this variation so that all three supporting players know where and when their colleague 10 needs them; they, of course, can then get in an early cross.

And of course everything worked on the left can also be coached on the right flank, and *vice versa*.

V · Crossing the ball into the penalty area

Crossing the ball into the penalty area will always be an important part of the game, but simply to get the ball in blindly is no longer enough. Players today must be more perceptive and aware of the wide range of crosses open to them. Players who get 'on the end' of a cross must not only be skilled at heading in its various forms, but must also realize that—in addition to the straightforward header at goal—many courses of action are open to them.

In the almost forgotten days of WM it was enough for a winger to sprint down the touch-line and hammer the ball across almost blindly. Then it was up to the big, bustling centre forward to fight with the stopper and opposing goalkeeper to get his headers in. Faced with the packed defences that we find today, further aided by improved goal-keeping, the old hopeful cross is outdated.

Years ago, the old-fashioned, six-foot-plus centre forward would call out, 'Far post', and, looking back, with the centre forward, centre half and goalkeeper all gathered in the region of the far post, one wonders how the uncovered area around the near post could have gone untapped for so long. The first time I saw a near-post cross was at West Ham, whose manager Ron Greenwood was the first to recognize the opportunities that lay there. Through his coaching, players like Geoff Hurst and Martin Peters scored goal after goal, confounding everyone for more than two years and making it seem so simple. Finally, other clubs began to see what West Ham were doing; while some were content to try and cover the exposed area, others copied West Ham by getting their players to drop in short centres aimed at the near post while colleagues off the ball made what have become known as near-post runs.

Goalkeepers expecting a high cross positioned themselves near the far post for a very good reason—simply because if the cross was short, it was far easier for them to go forward to meet the ball than it would have been for them to go backwards and try to jump if the ball flew over their heads. For just the same reason, the centre forward positioned himself 'far post' because he too could more easily go forward to meet the ball.

At corner kicks, the defending side always positioned a player at the near post. Even today, many of these defenders stand 'holding' the post, yet they are still not covering the danger area which lies some 6 yards or so away from the near post, around the edge of the goal area. Holding the post, the defender cannot reach the danger area in time if a good short cross is dropped in, combined with a good near-post run by a player who is adept—with head and foot—at turning these short crosses into goal.

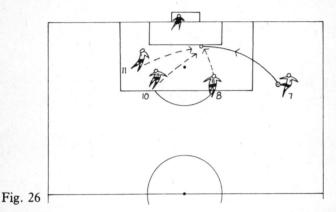

Fig. 26

In fluid play it is vital that the player crossing the ball should get the ball in early, before the defenders have time to organize themselves. In addition, it is preferable for the player making the near-post run (as in Fig. 26) to come from the left flank, the goalkeeper's blind side. Running across the defence, players 10 and 11 are much less likely to be spotted and picked up than player 8 would be, for example; but in favourable circumstances, when a quick counter-attack has caught the enemy with a depleted defence, there is no reason why any player should not be able to get in at the near post with a scoring chance. It is vital that the coach should explain to all the players that even full backs can get in near-post crosses, and that the ball is not passed direct to a player, but is dropped ahead into space 'for him' as he makes his run.

The coach must also stress that timing is vital. If a player on a near-post run makes his move too early and arrives in the scoring area before the ball, he should not hesitate, but should immediately 'check out'—run away—leaving the space for another player to make a run. If he does not check out, he will give the defender marking him time to catch him and mark him again; this defender will also be handily placed to prevent anyone else making a scoring attempt from this region. By checking out, with luck, the defender will follow his running opponent still further and open the space once more.

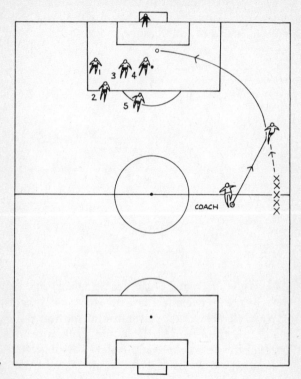

Fig. 27

As always, the coach will be best advised to practise this move in its simplest form, as in Fig. 27. (It follows, of course, that it is just as important to practise it with the ball played in from the left flank too.) The file of players XXXXX should be all the right-sided players (they will make near-post runs in their turn when the ball is fed in from the left): right back, right midfield and right wing, as well as the reserve team players in these positions. Players 1, 2, 3, 4, 5, etc. should be first- and second-team players, all starting their near-post runs from areas where they would normally be found in match play.

The coach starts the practice from around the position indicated, with a pass down the right and, in turn, the players from file X run on to the ball, looking up as they pursue it in order to pick their target, and play the ball in first time. Only if the ball is played in first time will the players making scoring attempts be able to time their runs and meet the ball just right. Here it may be of interest to relate an experience I had when first introducing players to this technique. An otherwise excellent player, a free goalscorer who later got many fine near-post goals, had a great deal of difficulty at first in timing his approach; he wanted to take off much too early. So, asking another player to feed the ball down the right, I transferred my attention to this player who was in fact the first-team left-sided striker. At first I tried talking to him, stressing that it was no good going yet because the other player was nowhere near ready to make his cross, but all to no avail. Finally, I had physically to restrain the player by holding both arms behind him very firmly and only letting go when I thought the moment was right. However, in time, he finally caught on and, as already stated, eventually scored many fine goals from around the near post.

Clearly, in match play, the defenders are not going to stand idly by and watch goals being scored at will, and the classic way of dealing with dangerous crosses is to make an attempt to cut them out. By getting a defender tight on the winger early, defences have always been able to severely limit the number of balls being played in. When wingers find that defenders stand off, positioning themselves in such a way that they are blocking with their bodies the direct flight of the ball into the near-post area, there are two simple ways of dealing with it; one requiring a particular skill, the other calling only for support.

Setting this up in practice, the coach gets the left back 3 to stand off the right winger 7 as he receives the ball (see Fig. 28a). At the same time a second player from the XXX file (in match play the right midfield or right back) is instructed to move up in support to receive an easy ball laid back by the winger. This player, 2 in the diagram, now plays the ball forward first time, lofting it into the air to pass over the heads of any intervening defenders and dropping it into the near-post region. Realizing that the cross cannot come in from the winger, the players out left, looking in turn for the chance to make scoring runs as the coach nominates them, wait until the ball has been played back and then time their runs accordingly.

It should perhaps be pointed out that perfection in getting the ball into the right spot when crossed is not, within reason, strictly necessary. A margin for error is built in here, for as the would-be scorer has to cover 15 or even maybe 20 yards to meet a very long cross, the runner has the opportunity to adjust his path to meet a ball slightly off course. Even if the ball comes in too low to be headed, the

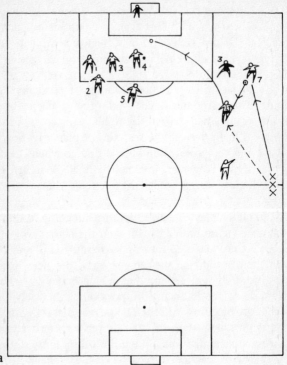

Fig. 28a

runner can take the ball on his chest and shoot with the second touch, or shoot first time with his foot.

When a defender tries to eliminate the cross by getting tight but standing off the winger, the first optional course is to try and curl or bend the ball around the defender. Most good players, given a little practice, should be able to do this. At first, however, particularly with less skilled players, no defender will relish the idea of standing in front of a winger who continually hammers the ball straight at him, hitting perhaps stomach and face and equally tender regions of the body. It will be advisable therefore to have some inanimate object to represent the defender, for example three corner flags planted, say, 6 inches apart. All the players in turn—left-sided players crossing from the left, right-sided players from the right—should try to curl the ball round the obstruction and drop it into the near-post area, starting with

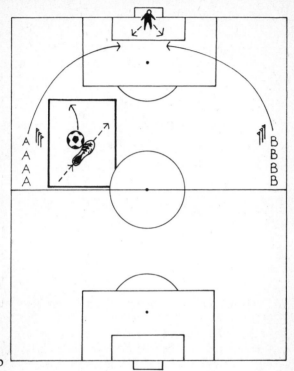

Fig. 28b

a dead ball. Later they should go on to receive a pass, controlling the ball with one touch and crossing it with the second touch, and then, finally, hit a moving ball first time round the object.

At first, as in Fig. 28b, it will probably be as well not to have runners looking for the ball but only two files of players, AAAA on the left and BBBB on the right, to cross the ball, curling it round the obstruction as illustrated with a goalkeeper to collect the balls as they come in and feed them back. The inset in Fig. 28b shows where the right foot, using the inside, should make contact with the ball to bend it, and the direction of the follow-through, which is vitally important.

Observation of match play reveals that defenders now are generally so aware of the dangers that exist around the near post that, for example, for corners and free kicks close to goal, the defending side positions a man directly opposite the near post on the goal area line as in Fig. 28c. One ploy that the attacking team can try here is to get a man (player 8 in Fig. 28c) who is not particularly good in the air, but is skilful and intelligent, to go and stand immediately in front of this defender. Getting there early, player 8 suddenly sprints towards the ball looking for a short pass and, very often, this will tempt the

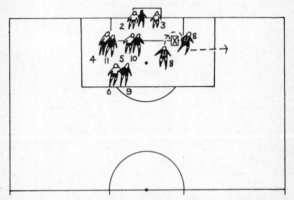

Fig. 28c

defender *X* to follow him, thus opening the way once more to the near post. If this move does not draw defender *X* out of position it will perhaps be a good idea if the player taking the kick makes a short pass to player 8. He should now be well placed with the ball at his feet to create a dangerous situation in the goal-mouth and if he does so, then perhaps the next time he tries to pull defender *X* away, he will be successful.

Though coaches and defenders now are generally fully aware of the danger represented by the near-post cross, I have seen numbers of goals, running well into three figures, scored from this move. Though it was a long time ago, probably the most important goal of this kind, in my opinion, will perhaps still be remembered. This came in the 1966 World Cup final when West Germany were leading England 1–0. As Fig. 29 roughly shows, Bobby Moore put his hand on the ball to take a free kick, looked up and played the ball up into space, as indicated, for Geoff Hurst to make a run from right to left and get in a header to score what looked like a simple goal. I well remember the

German goalkeeper, Hans Tilkowski, waving his arms, gesticulating and roaring at his defensive colleagues: 'How did he get in there unmarked?'

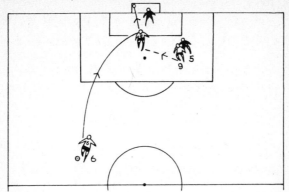

Fig. 29

That was a long time ago, but defenders still have not found the answer to the early ball accurately played in to the near post for a player running in from the far side, and timing his run just right. Probably they have failed to find an answer because there isn't one.

Other crosses

Although crosses aimed at the near post can be very profitable, this move should only be employed in favourable circumstances: when the goalkeeper is at or near the far post; when there is no defender covering the danger area; and when, in a position to get in a good early cross, another player is running into the near-post region. In any case, the game would become very boring if every attack ended with a near-post cross, though it should be employed when the players concerned think they can score. But other crosses can also bring rewards if a little thought and practice is given to the various types of centre.

First, however, it is as well to consider that most goalkeepers nowadays stand six foot or over and, if they have reached professional standard, they will surely be very competent at dealing with high balls. Even at a lower level of the game, it is essential for goalkeepers to be able to deal with high crosses and most of them can be expected to reach a good standard. Given these facts about goalkeepers—their height and ability in the air—it has to be accepted that almost anything put high into the six-yard area will be a goalkeeper's ball, except for the area already mentioned: around and short of the near post.

To bring results, therefore, corner kicks should be delivered into the three zones—marked 1, 2 and 3 in Fig. 30—beyond the reach of the average goalkeeper, against a really top-class goalkeeper who excels in the air they should even be a shade further out than this. Generally, however, with penalty areas as crowded as they are today,

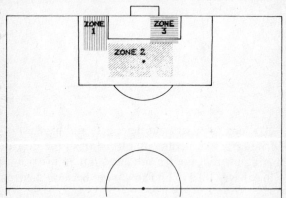

Fig. 30

high balls delivered into these three zones as marked will present problems for the goalkeeper since, with friend and foe obstructing him, he will have considerable difficulty in getting out of them, however good he is. So high crosses should be aimed into one of these three zones and it follows that crosses got in early stand a better chance of bringing rewards. Zone 3, the near-post area, has of course already been covered, so we shall now concentrate on zones 1 and 2.

No one can say with certainty that a high cross aimed at any particular zone will reach its mark for that would demand an unreasonably high degree of accuracy and technical skill from the player crossing the ball. Sometimes, of course, they will go in exactly right, but crosses can only be aimed to reach a general area within a particular zone, and therefore it follows that as many attacking players as possible should be ready to meet a cross in each zone. Zone 2, for example, should be given to at least three attacking players, spread out rather than bunched together, perhaps positioning themselves so that with arms extended they can just reach each other with their fingertips—or nearly. They should try to time their run-up to the ball just right to allow a one-footed take-off that will give them the highest possible jump.

For corner kicks and free kicks close to goal, most teams place their players who can head the ball best beyond zone 2 but running into it, hoping that in so doing they will be able to shake off anyone trying to mark them and be ready to take off from their best foot. In fluid play probably only the two central strikers will be handily placed to make a run into zone 2; but Fig. 31a, showing the situation as for corner kicks etc., includes the stopper 5 also making a run across this zone.

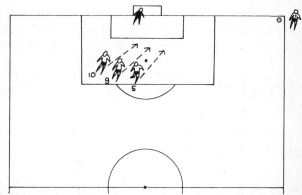

Fig. 31a

In match play, any player close enough to make a run into zone 2 looking for the chance to head at goal should, of course, be encouraged to do so; in practice, therefore, we may find any or all of the midfield players in this zone to supplement the central strikers. As long as the cross is not delivered into an area where the goalkeeper can reach it, to catch the ball or punch it away, the chances of making a good header at goal must be considered quite high. Players cannot be expected to score every time, but everyone who meets the ball in this zone in the air should attempt a direct header at goal, hitting the ball as powerfully as possible.

The elements involved here—good crosses, with skilled headers of the ball making good runs to produce a high proportion of headed balls on target to bring a number of goals—are all part of the coach's work. Having organized the heading attacks in zone 2 and worked at crosses and headers in zone 3, he should thus go on to make sure that the approach is orderly and intelligent and flexible instead—as with many teams (even professional)—of being haphazard and very largely left to luck. Hoping that things will happen is no way for a good coach to approach the game. He cannot plan everything, but he can organize things in an intelligent way and coach his players in practice to make good runs looking for headers at goal, and improve their ability at crossing and heading.

When a cross arrives at head height in zone 1, whether by accident through poor performance or by design, it cannot really be considered a scoring chance since the angle from which the header must be delivered, and the position of the goalkeeper narrowing that angle, make it very difficult indeed to score. If such a ball drops below heading height, perhaps the best solution is to drive it hard into the goal-mouth, hoping for a deflection into goal. However, the only real way to beat a good goalkeeper from such an angle with a header is to try to propel the ball high over the goalkeeper and drop it down behind him into the goal, as in Fig. 31b. But this is a very difficult skill to acquire and there is a much better alternative.

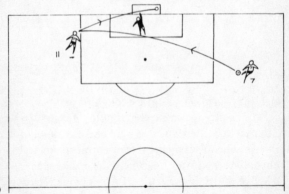

Fig. 31b

The practice illustrated in Fig. 31c shows the coach using his left winger 11 and left back 3 to meet a stream of long crosses from the right wing (players 7, 2 and 4—the right winger, right back, and right midfield—should be coached to deal with crosses coming from the left wing). But the players in file XXX will send over crosses in turn and the coach will nominate the left-sided players 3 and 11 in turn to make a run and meet each cross, instructing them **to head the ball back across the face of the goal.** Players 2, 7 and 4 can be used in file XXX,

Fig. 31c

and after ten minutes of crossing from the right, the practice can be switched to the other flank.

In the centre, the coach can place players 8, 9, 10, 5 and 6 who might all be expected in match play to be in heading situations close to goal in zone 2. Initially they will not be involved because the crosses from either flank will fly high over their heads. When the crosses come from the right wing, all the players in zone 2 will be facing that way, looking for the chance to score with a direct header. They should be instructed that every time the ball flies high over their heads they should immediately turn to face it as it is headed back across goal from the left, positioning themselves with their right shoulder pointed towards goal so that they will be right for a header at goal, or alternatively a left-footed volley at goal if the ball drops low before them (it will be a right-footed volley if the initial cross comes from the left wing and is headed back).

Bad balls

Finally, because not all crosses will drop nicely in the zones aimed for, allowance must be made for bad balls. All bad balls can be turned into good balls if the players are alive and react quickly; and crosses are no exception.

Fig. 32a shows an intended near-post cross that is so wide of the target that untouched it would go off for a goal kick. If the near-post runner is alert and quick enough, he can change the direction of his run and head the ball back, away from goal, for a colleague to shoot first time.

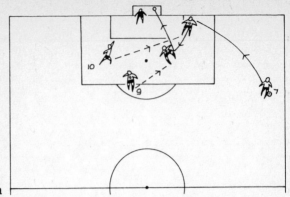

Fig. 32a

In Fig. 32b a poor cross aimed at zone 2 arrives much too far out, on or about the edge of the penalty area. Again, players 8, 9, 10, 5 and 6 all have the chance to head (or chest) the ball down for player 4 to come up and shoot at goal.

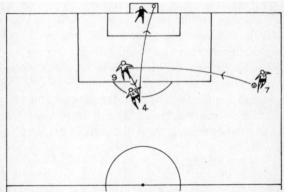

Fig. 32b

In Fig. 32c the longer cross aimed beyond the goal into zone 1 is over-hit or screwed; untouched, it too would go off for a goal kick. There will be no chance of scoring here and players making runs into this area hoping for a good cross will have trouble reaching the ball; but perhaps they can, with their head or maybe by using an overhead kick, pull the ball back away from goal—again for a colleague to shoot.

All these options are open to the players if the coach makes them aware of them. In practice there will be ample opportunity, when

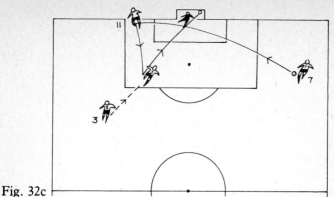

Fig. 32c

crosses go wide of their target, to try and convert bad crosses into shooting chances in the manner just described.

As with everything else, practice makes perfect. Timing of the runs to meet crosses, heading and shooting skills, as well as ability in crossing the ball are all vital, integral parts of the game, and the coach should see that his players work at them all. Last but not least, it should be understood that although most of the figures illustrate attacks developing on the right flank, the coach should also set up all practices coming from the left wing, reversing everything that is inapplicable to left-wing centres.

VI · *Throws-in*

Statistics show that throws-in are far more common than either corners or free kicks close to goal (discussed in the next chapter). In coaching, the right balance should be found between these two aspects of the attacking game, and more attention should be given to the throw-in, potentially of greater value in terms of goals, than it is at present.

A count taken during the full ninety minutes of a First Division game revealed the following facts:

	Throws-in	Corners	Free kicks near goal
Home team	44	7	5
Away team	21	1	1

The fact that the home team had the advantage of twice as many throws-in, and relatively many more corners and free kicks near goal, is not to me the most important factor—this is what would be expected in the modern game in which away teams are the more defensive. The interesting fact is the totals of the two teams:

Throws-in	Corners	Free kicks near goal
65	8	6

Next week the away team will normally be at home and the figures will be reversed. This is why the overall totals are most interesting, because they show that on average a team can expect eight times as many throws-in as corner kicks.

Present thinking on throws-in has resulted in two throws in particular becoming quite commonplace. The one described in Fig. 33a is seen very often when the throw-in takes place on or about the halfway line or further back; Fig 33b shows an attempt to turn a throw-in near the enemy goal into a corner-type attack, and is seen just as often.

In Fig. 33a, all the players who could receive the ball from a throw-in are marked, particularly those who are goal-side of the throw and could break away if not covered. But when a full back drops back

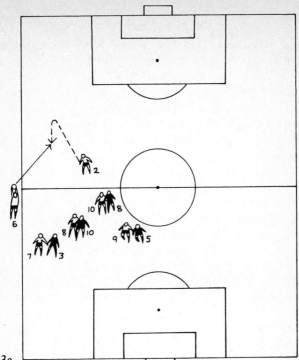

Fig. 33a

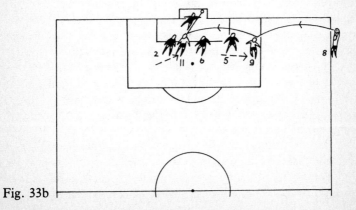

Fig. 33b

towards his own goal, most teams are reluctant to put a player out of the game by marking him. Instead they concede possession and concentrate on marking everyone that the full back, number 2 in Fig. 33a, could pass to. From there, it is of course possible to *play* the ball, but all too often, particularly with British teams, the next move is a long, high ball up the middle which leads nowhere. It is, however, a good throw for teams that are prepared to be patient and build up their attacks, for when the full back is left completely free of opposition, possession can be guaranteed from the throw-in, and that is better than nothing.

The second throw-in is used particularly by those teams who have a long-throw specialist, though my observations lead me to the conclusion that most long throws are in fact foul throws. However, it is a fact that players get away with them, perhaps because they usually take a run-up before throwing and the sheer speed of the movement deceives the officials. Near the corner flag, the long throw is directed on to the head of a player who comes to meet the ball, as described in Fig. 33b, and he heads it on across the face of the goal.

I personally dislike this particular throw because the player heading the ball is doing so 'blind'. He *hopes* that someone will be well placed to turn his back-header into goal. It has to be admitted that it sometimes works, but I prefer a little more reliance on judgement and a lot less on luck. Elsewhere I have recommended a header across goal, but this follows an over-hit corner or cross from the wing when the player heading the ball back has his colleagues in front of him and, exercising his judgement as well as his heading skill, can aim for a man that he can see.

Before going on to describe the throws-in that I prefer, based on skill and timing, this seems to be an appropriate point to mention a defensive ploy that used to be commonplace but has now virtually disappeared. Fig. 34 shows the most frequently seen throw-in of all. Any two players can use this throw, but here player 6 throws the ball in to player 8 who is marked but is moving towards the ball and can therefore get one touch to the ball before he is challenged. Player 8 simply passes the ball straight back to the thrower, player 6, and the game goes on from there.

A great many teams still use this throw as a basic move, but the ploy I advocate, that I haven't seen for years, is to get the winger of the team that is not taking the throw, player 7, to drop back and put himself between the player taking the throw and the man receiving it. It will

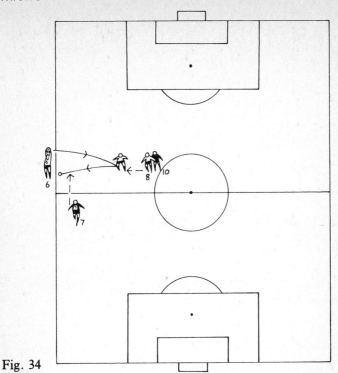

Fig. 34

not always work, but very often one used to see this winger nicking the ball when the throw turned out to be a one-two—and when the timing of his run was spot-on. When it works, defence is turned into attack in a fraction of a second and, if possession of the ball is not won by interception, the winger is very nicely placed to harass the thrower when he receives the ball back.

Turning now to the creative aspect of throws-in, one throw-in that is well worth trying involves the simple cross-over of two midfield players, or a midfield player with a striker. In Fig. 35 two midfield players, 8 and 10, are involved, using the old basic principle that players who are short should go long and players who are long should come short. As the thrower 6 is shaping up to take the throw, player 8, who is positioned closer to the enemy goal, sprints towards him. His marker will be after him of course, but as 8 had the advantage in that he could choose the moment to go, his opponent will be a little behind

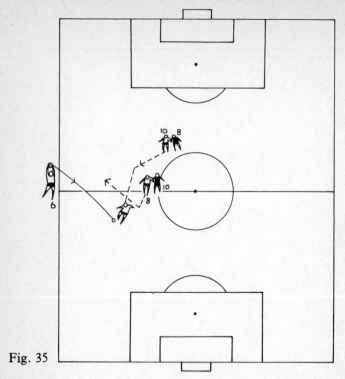

Fig. 35

him. However, it is not the opponent that is of interest, but the space that 8 and his marker have just vacated. Player 10, coming from a fairly deep position and running quite hard towards the thrower as a feint, can now judge his moment correctly and, though marked (and naturally followed), can sprint away into the space just vacated by player 8 to receive a well-timed throw from player 6.

A similar move with an extra twist involves wingers. In Fig. 36, right winger 7, who is positioned say 30 yards from the thrower, suddenly sprints towards him. If the man marking him, left back 3, declines to follow and tight-mark him, then right winger 7 should receive a ball at his feet that he can turn with. More likely, however, left back 3 will go with 7, staying as tight as he can all the way, and this opens the door to a player coming from the area level with the thrower

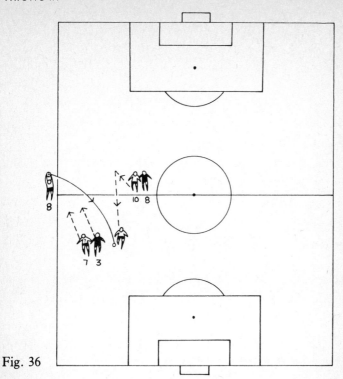

Fig. 36

to break away down the right. This is a variation of the move in Fig. 35 but played lengthways up and down the pitch.

But the throw-in I really advocate is one that I have seen performed only very rarely, and then perhaps by players who didn't even realize what they were doing. This is described in Fig. 37 (a, b and c), and I suggest that the most time be given to it in training because, when it is carried out well, it is infallible. Looking first at Fig. 37a, which shows only one man and the thrower, the advantage will be more clearly seen. Here player 10 is positioned in midfield, marked by an opponent who is goal-side of him as defenders always try to be. As the thrower 4 shapes up to take the throw, player 10 makes a run angled across the pitch but generally away from his own goal. Having got the man marking him on the move, chasing after him as hard as he can, he now suddenly checks and turns away from his opponent who, being goal-side, will still be on his left. Turning to the right, player 10 now wants

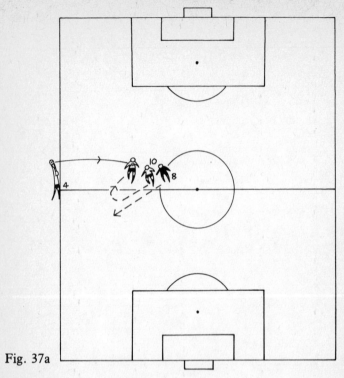

Fig. 37a

the ball delivered precisely and immediately to the outside of his left foot because no matter how the opponent reacts, this ball is *on the screening side of player 10*.

Having gained possession of the ball, player 10 now has many options open to him. If he has gained a yard on his opponent, or knows from previous experience that he has the beating of this particular individual, he can take him on and go by him. But even if the opponent has a personal edge and is still there on the 10's right, possession is retained because, with the ball on the outside of his left foot, 10 is screening the ball with his body from a challenge. From here he can lay the ball off using the outside of his left foot to any colleague in support, or he can even make a long crossfield pass for his left winger to drop back to, or for his colleague at left back to advance to. These options are shown in Fig. 37b. Whatever happens, if the

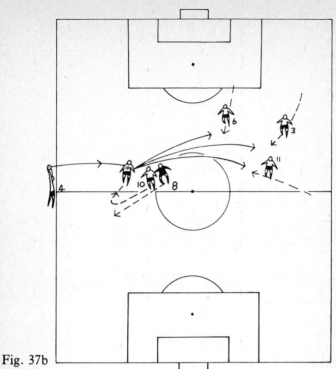

Fig. 37b

throw is accurate and well timed, turning away from the man marking him puts player 10 into a very good position.

In Fig. 37c several players in the midfield region are all making runs similar to player 10's in Fig. 37a and at different moments of their own individual choice they each turn away, giving the thrower ample opportunity to pick out a runner who looks particularly well placed with regard to his marker; as that man makes his *turn away* from his opponent, the thrower just drops the ball in, nice and sweet.

Fig. 37c also shows the right winger 7. If he makes a run back towards the thrower his marker, the left back 3, will most likely be on either his left or his right. If 7 suddenly checks and turns away from his man, then he, too, has put himself into a favourable position to receive the ball in such a way that his body will screen it from his opponent and he can even break away.

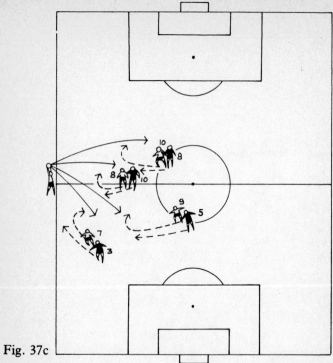

Fig. 37c

VII · *Free kicks and corner kicks*

Many coaches place emphasis on coaching corners and free kicks close to the enemy goal largely because a little time spent on working out a good idea may often bring a quick reward in the shape of a goal in next week's match. Coaching set pieces is also attractive to coaches working with small boys or amateurs who do not train very often or for very long. But in these circumstances I would prefer to devote all the available time to coaching approach play, for that is basic to the game.

In my view, too much rubbish has been spoken and written about 'missed scoring chances'. I have two points to make on this theme:

1. It is the quality of the chance that counts.
2. It is the quality of the attacking player's skill that is important.

With regard to the first point, I believe that thirty or forty high balls thumped into the enemy penalty area are not scoring chances, but only half-chances at best. Real chances are those created by penetrating the enemy penalty area by keeping the ball low and playing it in to the feet of a player in a shooting position. As to the second, I have seen too many real chances missed, or taken at the second attempt (for example when the enemy goalkeeper half stops the shot, and the shooting player gets a second chance at the loose ball). It is the first chance that should be put into the net, but examples of second-chance goals serve to prove my belief that the skill of attacking players needs to be improved by practice. The greater the finishing skill of an attacking player, the higher the percentage of real chances he will score from, as shown by Gerd Müller, the West German centre forward until after the 1974 World Cup. Müller very rarely missed chances because he had a very high degree of skill with either foot.

Having said that, it still remains a fact that corner kicks and free kicks do give the attacking team the opportunity to create a scoring chance, so most coaches will want to deal with them. Taking corner kicks first, I would like to stress that unless the attacking team possesses an extremely good header of the ball, who is tall and jumps well, then, against a well-organized defence with three, or perhaps four, good headers of the ball plus a first-class goalkeeper who comes well out for high crosses, corner kicks will produce a relatively low number of goals. If corners do bring goals, it is more likely to be because of defensive errors. In my view, this is taking a negative approach to the game.

I should prefer to approach a corner kick as small boys do. Because young boys usually cannot kick the ball into the goal-mouth from the corner flag, and because boys under sixteen years are rarely good and confident headers of the ball, youngsters tend to take short corner kicks. From there they attempt to work the ball into the penalty area by inter-passing, or dribbling and inter-passing, trying to create a shooting position for someone. That is the approach I should like to see, because then the advantages that accrue to teams with four big defenders, all good headers of the ball, are nullified.

This does not mean that a team with a player in the mould of Tommy Lawton, who could jump so well that I once saw him get above the height of the cross bar and head the ball 'down' into goal, should not use his talent. Torres, of Benfica and Portugal, who came much later, was another player who was very tall and very good in the air. But lacking such players who are exceptionally good in the air in front of goal, and bearing in mind the advantages in favour of the defenders, I do not think that the orthodox high centre from a corner kick brings much reward.

But if coaches insist on trying to score with high crosses from corners, then at least try to organize something in favour of the attacking team. The player taking the corner kick cannot guarantee one hundred per cent accuracy with his kicks. Proof of this is the fact that such kicks sometimes end up in the roof of the net, out of play. So it follows that the kicker can only *try* to float the ball across in a general line. Bearing this in mind, the coach should place the team's best headers in the positions of players 9, 10 and 11 in Fig. 38a. Obviously this move can be worked off left-wing corners, too, and these should also be practised. The idea is that, by forming up in line abreast and sprinting across the penalty area to meet the ball at the right moment, one of the three attacking players will find the ball passing close enough to be headed at goal. Sprinting across the penalty area means that the players should be able to meet the ball in the air after a one-footed take-off on the run, thus gaining maximum height. It also means that they will be very difficult to mark.

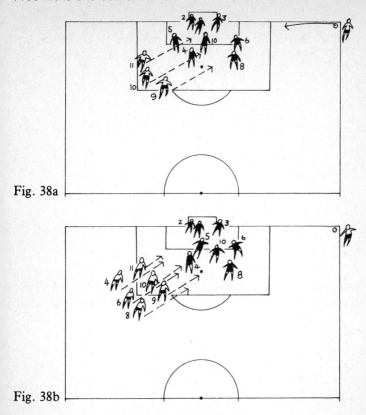

Fig. 38a

Fig. 38b

   Another alternative method of distributing the attacking players is
shown in Fig. 38b. This makes allowance for the fact that in the move
shown in Fig. 38a timing the run across goal is essential, for while one
of the three players might be perfectly positioned in terms of space, he
might be out with regard to time and find the ball passing over his
head. In Fig. 38b the second wave of players, 4, 6 and 8, need not
necessarily be outstanding jumpers, for the first wave, 9, 10 and 11,
will have attracted the big men in the defence. One of the second
wave, though not a good jumper and not especially big, may find that
he is in just the right place in terms of space and time, and is relatively
free to make a good header at goal.
   This approach is, I believe, better than simply spreading the attacking players around the penalty area at random, for this often leads to
two (or more) players trying to head the ball at the same time and only

succeeding in putting each other off. There is the added possibility that each of two possible heading players will leave the ball to the other, and the opportunity to get a header in will be lost.

The near-post cross, already mentioned in Chapter V, can be productive at corners, given an extra twist. Many defences now position a reliable defender on the corner of the 6-yard line nearest the ball at corner kicks to guard against a near-post header—as shown in Fig. 39a. In this situation I have found that, if I get one of my most skilful players (10 in the figure) to go and stand, say, 1 yard in front of this defender (6 here) and then, after a moment, suddenly to sprint away towards the corner flag, calling for a short pass, he can often pull player 6 towards him. This temporarily frees the near-post area and player 11, or anyone else running from the blind side of the defence, as in Fig. 39b, can get in unmarked to meet a near-post cross if one is given at the right time.

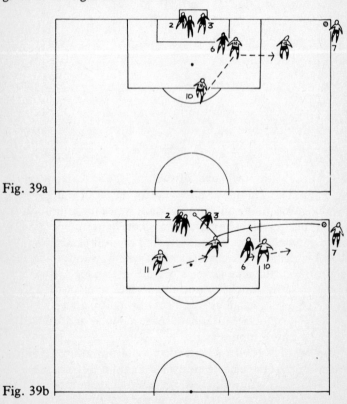

Fig. 39a

Fig. 39b

Corner kicks may well excite the crowds, but I find them rather dull because either they can be crossed high into the goal-mouth, or they can be taken short. There is no other choice. Free kicks close to goal are much more interesting because of the variety of ideas that can be brought into play here. The possibilities are almost without limit, and at any time a *new kick* may be seen that is the product of a thoughtful coach or the inspiration of an intelligent player.

The basic rule about taking free kicks close to goal is the same as for fluid play—look and think, then act. The added advantage here is that though the situation can change as players fly about, the player(s) taking the kick have time for thought.

Dealing first with direct free kicks—that is to say, free kicks from which a goal can be scored direct, without the ball having to touch another player—the simplest, yet perhaps the most skilful, is the straightforward chip over the defensive wall, or the shot curled round the wall. For either of these, a player of very great skill is required to take the kick, though the necessary skills can be acquired with constant practice.

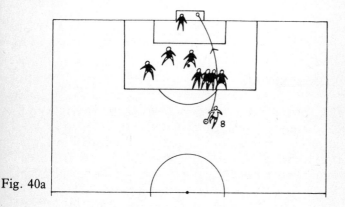

Fig. 40a

The chip over the wall is described in Fig. 40a. Taken by player 8, it is flighted over the wall, dipping later, and is intended to enter the goal below the bar and inside the post near the angle where they meet. The player taking the kick has to 'dig' his big toe into the turf and really get underneath the ball without following through. This skill must be mastered first.

To curl the ball around the wall is, if anything, more difficult than chipping it. Player 8 in Fig. 40b has to get his kicking foot underneath the ball, using the area of his big toe to give it *lift*. In addition he has to kick across the back of the ball with a *slicing* of the side of his instep, and then follow through, wrapping his right foot around the ball as it departs. This again requires a skill that must be acquired and takes a lot of practice. The intention is for the ball to go over and around the end man in the wall, and, having done so, to curl back in flight to the region of the near post.

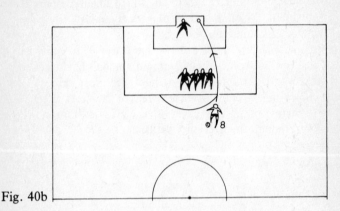

Fig. 40b

To underline the fact that ideas can be adapted to suit the limited skills of less skilled players, let us take a few minutes to think about free kicks close to the enemy goal. Many skilful players must have impressed everyone with their ability to swerve or chip a dead ball around, or over, a line of defenders set up as a wall to face a direct free kick close to their penalty area. The West German star Gunter Netzer was a prime example of a player able to exploit this situation, but he had exceptional skill. A team of less skilled players will often have no one who can reproduce the same ability with a dead ball. However, thinking a little further about the situation it will become clear that it is much easier to chip or swerve a ball that is rolling towards him nicely. So we can make it possible for a player to use his more limited skill at a free kick by moving the ball for him.

Fig. 40c shows a free kick just outside the enemy penalty area with the defending side erecting a defensive wall. We need two players to position themselves as described, each looking as if they might take the kick. At the signal from the referee, player A moves forward as if to take the kick, but stepping over the ball, turns and rolls it back nicely for player B, some 5 yards back, to impart swerve to the ball by using the inside of his right foot and cutting underneath the ball—as in a table-tennis shot. Though the shot is in fact taken from 5 yards further back than Netzer would have taken it, there is an advantage now that the defensive wall will have broken up, with players flying about in all directions, probably helping to obscure the goalkeeper's sight of the ball.

Fig. 40c

Some of the more spectacular free kicks that I have seen myself, most of which can be used regardless of whether the kick is direct or indirect, may perhaps be mentioned here. The first I witnessed in the Brazil v Czechoslovakia World Cup game in Mexico, during the 1970 competition. The Czechs conceded a free kick just outside the penalty area right in front of goal and a line of defenders made a wall, supervised by the Czech goalkeeper Ivo Viktor who left himself with half the goal to defend, most of it to his right-hand side, as in Fig. 41. Pelé, number 10, picked up the ball and placed it very carefully before retracing his steps and surveying the situation, looking as if he were about to take the kick. Meanwhile, Rivelino, 11, had been very careful to stay out of the goalkeeper's sight, mingling with Czech players and standing finally in such a way that he had the Czech's defensive wall between himself and the goal. Clearly this had been very well rehearsed, for now two things happened, in quick succession. First, Jairzinho, 7, appeared from nowhere, very late, to put himself on the end of the Czech wall as indicated. Then number 11, Rivelino, made

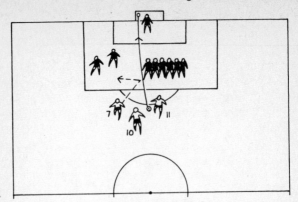

Fig. 41

his run up to the ball, approaching it from an angle of almost 90 degrees to the goal and ball. Fractionally before he hit it with real power, Jairzinho ran to get out of the way and the ball whooshed through the gap. Rivelino had aimed to hit the ball straight at Jairzinho so that Viktor didn't get a good look at it, and the goalkeeper was beaten low down to his right hand.

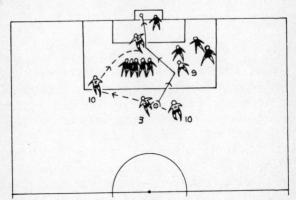

Fig. 42

Another very good, but much more complicated, free kick, described in Fig. 42, was taken by Bulgaria in their match against Peru in that same World Cup competition. The three Bulgarian players directly involved in what was obviously another very well-rehearsed affair were inside left Dermendiev, 10, left back Aladjov, 3, and centre forward Jekov, 9. The Peruvian defenders constructed a five-man wall while their goalkeeper positioned himself to cover the other half of the goal. More Peruvian players spread themselves around the penalty area as shown. The three key Bulgarians positioned themselves as follows: Dermendiev and Aladjov stood behind the ball, apparently discussing what to do, while Jekov mingled with the Peruvian defenders. Dermendiev then moved up as if to take a shot, stepped over the ball, moved left, and stopped. Next came Aladjov, running at the ball as if he were going to break the net but instead he pushed a firm ball into the space to the left of the defensive wall as indicated. Jekov was sprinting to meet this pass, reached the ball first, and first time stabbed it into the space behind the wall. Now came Dermendiev again, timing his run so that he was on-side to pick up the ball off Jekov, run forward with the ball, and then shoot into the net. The key factor here, that permitted the Bulgarians to get away with this kick so easily, was that Peru left no free man to cover space and pick up a runner on Bulgaria's left wing. But for it to work, Jekov also had to be first to the ball when Aladjov placed it in space.

It is interesting to note that in this game Bulgaria were awarded another free kick soon afterwards in a similar position, and the Peru goalkeeper was so unsettled by what the Bulgarians had done that he appeared to be very nervous indeed. So much so that at this second kick a direct shot took him by surprise and, after getting both hands to the ball, he allowed it to spin over his right shoulder into the goal.

Fig. 43

On returning from Mexico, I coached this free kick with some success, but knowing that it could be countered if a free player was kept in defence where Peru's right back should have been, I also added a variation for such occasions, as in Fig. 43. I used players 8 and

9 as the men apparently talking over the ball while my right winger 7 positioned himself just a yard in front of the defensive wall. Any player trying to get amongst the players in the wall would be jostled and held if he tried to move, so it is important that 7 should be in front of the wall. First, player 8 stepped up to take the kick, but passed over the ball and moved into space as indicated. Then, immediately behind him, so as to waste no time, player 9 followed up and gave a firm pass to 7, who laid the ball off first time into space for 9. This player now had a full view of the enemy goal and was able to place his shot into the unprotected half left by the goalkeeper for the wall to cover.

Now follow a few ideas for free kicks that I have seen carried out successfully at various matches. In Fig. 44 a short pass is used to change the angle of the shot at goal by using a square pass into space. This allows player 8 in the diagram to receive a short pass from player 4, and then shoot through the space behind the defensive wall into the goalkeeper's now unprotected right-hand corner.

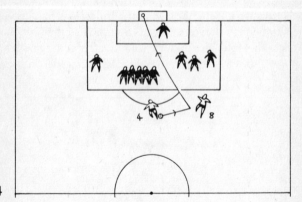

Fig. 44

The free kicks described in Fig. 45a, for the left wing, and Fig. 45b, for the right, are exactly the same in principle, but only serve to underline that what can be worked on one flank can also succeed on the other side of the field. This ploy is always worth trying if the defenders line up with a wall, but leave a space in what should be the right back's zone (see Fig. 45a). Here player 10 shapes up to take a direct shot at goal, but the left back 3, well placed upfield, comes sprinting late into that space to take a short pass beyond the wall.

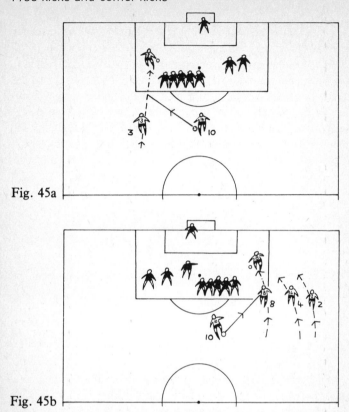

Fig. 45a

Fig. 45b

From there the left back can either try to work a shooting position for himself, can try to find space in front of an oncoming colleague who has broken from the ruck of loose players, or can simply drive the ball hard into the goal-mouth hoping for a deflection into goal. Although it might appear that the end man on the wall could have cut off the pass, or have sprinted after the left back, in fact the players in the defensive wall usually hold each other so tight to prevent gaps appearing through which a player with an accurate shot can shoot that the end man would have found it difficult to break free. Obviously the players used in the kicks described in Figs. 45a and b can be varied according to who is best placed to break away on the flank and get round the wall looking for a pass. Timing of the run is important too, for the runner must always look across the pitch and ensure that he does not go too early, or run into an off-side position.

Fig. 46 describes a free kick that could be regarded as a variation of
the kick taken by Rivelino in the 1970 World Cup. Here an intelligent
attacking player puts himself on the 'outside' end of the defensive wall
and because he appears not to represent any danger he will not
normally be interfered with or jostled. Timing to guard against an
off-side decision is the key here, for player 10, placed on the end of the
wall, must turn away and sprint to catch the ball exactly a fraction of a
second after the kick has been taken. For the player taking the kick
(player 8 here), the problem is how to get the ball into the space

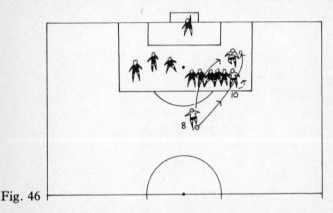

Fig. 46

required by 10. He can either go over the wall with a chip or go round
the end with a curled pass along the ground. Either way, player 10
should be through into a shooting position if he is found with a good
ball and turns to sprint towards goal at just the right moment.

None of these free kicks is difficult to coach. Simply ask the players
in practice to follow the movements of Jairzinho and Rivelino; Dermendiev, Jekov and Aladjov, as described in the figures above. After
the session, the coach could profitably ask his players if anyone has
any ideas of their own, either completely new, or slight variations of
the kicks just practised. If a player comes up with a good idea, then try
it, and add it to the team's repertoire if it works.

Then—very important—the coach should ask his defenders,
'What are we going to do if someone tries to work these free kicks
against us?' For me, the last part is the heart of coaching, for as
coaches we must involve the players. In every situation we are trying
to get our attacking players to attempt good moves and create shooting
positions, and we are also trying to get our defenders to think logically

about the problems they encounter in match play and to help them overcome the difficulties and to find answers.

One last thought on free kicks in potential goal-producing situations: at one time it was possible to take free kicks quickly, but today the defensive players illegally delay the taking of free kicks—by stealing the ball, and also by refusing to get back the statutory 10 yards until the referee forces them to do so. It is to be hoped that at some time in the future, referees will become more strict and stamp out both these practices, handing out yellow cards for first offenders and red cards for a player who commits the same offence twice. If and when that day comes, the players should be encouraged to try, as the old-timers once did, to get in a quick shot, or to make a quick pass as soon as the referee indicates they are clear to take the kick. Morally, the free kick is a punishment for an offence by the defending side, but officials allow the offending side to gain as much advantage as possible before the kick is taken. Clearly this is wrong, for the advantage should go to the attacking team, and if circumstances allow, the players should be quick to take advantage of any opportunity that arises.

VIII · *The one-two or wall pass*

The one-two or wall pass, as it is known amongst British coaches (the double pass in most European countries) is the first step towards combined play. In the days of open football, in the 1930s, teams like Austria, Hungary and Czechoslovakia excelled at it, and were very good indeed to watch. As the game has become more defensive, the one-two has become more difficult to play, particularly close to and inside the enemy penalty area. But with coaching and encouragement, there is no reason why players should not learn to play the one-two near to their own goal. It is simple, it is intelligent, and with just a little thought it works.

Arthur Rowe, the highly successful manager–coach of Tottenham Hotspur in their heyday around 1950–1, played one-twos every-where. Spurs at that time were known as the 'push and run team'— which perhaps should have been amended to 'push and run, *looking for the ball back*'. Even in the 1960s West Ham United built their attacks from the back by intelligent football in which the one-two played a big part. If West Ham could make it work in England, then there is no valid reason why other teams should not do it today for, in terms of defence, the English game has not changed since Bobby Moore, Martin Peters, Ronnie Boyce and Johnny Byrne were at their best for West Ham. On the international scene, as late as 1970, before they lost the last of their great forwards Pelé and Tostao, the Brazilians excelled at playing one-twos and even pulled them off as they went into the box to shoot.

Playing the ball out of defence is still very easy if one-twos are used, even in the late 1970s. This will not change either, for even the most defence-minded team falls back in strength towards its own goal, leaving virtually only the strikers (who are outnumbered) to make a token attempt to win the ball back. In midfield it gets slightly more difficult because the opposition there offers a greater challenge in terms of numbers, but it is still relatively easy to play the double pass if the players are well coached. Even going into the enemy penalty area, skilful and intelligent players can often pull off a one-two against the most ruthless and destructive defence.

It is so much more desirable to play the ball out of defence than merely to use a long kick. Observation shows that this usually gets headed or kicked straight back. By playing the ball from man to man (including using the one-two), players are able to get the ball well into the enemy half before producing the final penetrating pass.

In the 1978 World Cup, little Peru excelled with attacking football on the floor. Given one outstanding player in Cubillas, another very good player in Cueta, and others around them who understood what was going on, they proved themselves able to take Scotland apart. Peru deserved a better fate in 1978 if only for the quality of their attacking football, but clearly they had a great inferiority complex about playing against Brazil and Argentina. So far as Brazil was concerned, Peru's real football skills in fact left them far behind, but they lacked a big strong central striker like Mario Kempes of Argentina, and were also weak in defence. Kempes and their inferiority complex, with the addition of an occasional touch of madness from their own goalkeeper, were enough to destroy Peru's chances.

But with good skills, good coaching, and intelligent players who can beat a man with a feint, take on another with a dribble, and then produce a successful one-two, even the most solid European defences could be put in jeopardy. In any case, what enjoyment there lies in good football, for both players and spectators!

The simplest practice for developing the knack of the one-two is to have a little game of keep-ball, two against two, in, say, the penalty area. In turns, every player can have a go at it, four at a time, but the coach should first show the players the three essential ingredients for good one-twos.

Golden rule number one is simple: do not let an opponent get too close to the ball before playing it off. With an opponent rushing at him, the player with the ball can easily circumvent the challenger with a good pass, but take care that the challenger is not close enough to deflect the ball, or even 'nick it' completely.

Rule number two is also simple but not so easy to acquire. The player receiving the ball *must* turn his body sideways so that his shoulders are pointing towards the two goals. Then simply by turning his head he can reconsider the situation, which can change in a fraction of a second. If an intelligent opponent is close enough, and has anticipated the return pass, then the player receiving the ball will know (because he has looked) if it is safe for him to turn on the ball and keep it momentarily. Alternatively, if the player receiving the first pass sees that one opponent is coming on his back to challenge, while another is running to cut off the second pass in the one-two, then he can play the ball back easily to an unmarked player in defence, who will try again to begin a good build-up.

If a well-coached team plays the ball around like this, the opposition will soon tire of chasing shadows for they will be eager to conserve their energy. So even if they cannot go forward at once, keeping the ball for perhaps a minute at a time, trying to build up a good attack, will eventually deter the opposition from wasting precious energy on what they are now learning from experience is only a lot of fruitless chasing.

Golden rule number three is a little more difficult to get across to players, a very high percentage of whom play naturally. But a good coach will explain that the man who makes the first pass now becomes the 'runner', looking for the return pass, and it is the runner who *dictates* where the return pass must be laid to complete the one-two. Thus the runner must run *at space*, and this applies in defence just as much as in attack. The spaces that a player can run at are relatively easy to find in defence, a little more difficult to find in the build-up to the enemy goal, and it requires highly skilled and well-coached players to find the slightest space in the enemy penalty area—and to make successful use of it.

To become really good at one-twos, the penalty area can be used to accommodate three players v three and four v four, with a one-touch rule added later. This will make the players think and really leap about to get free in support of their colleague who has the ball. Good players could go even further and play six v six inside the box, if they are well coached and skilful. Then in match play, when they have the whole pitch to play in, the one-two game seems to be easy.

To reiterate. If I have the ball at left back and pass the ball to the left midfield, I must immediately sprint into a space where there is no opponent who can get there in time to stop me getting the ball back.

Having explained the three golden rules and demonstrated that the runner dictates, the players can be left, according to their standard, to play one-touch football in the penalty area while the coach works with the strikers and attacking midfield players at the other end of the playing area or training ground.

In Fig. 47a we have a typical British back four. It will probably help the players to understand the problem and the principle about running at space if the coach sets up this attack. Player 8 has possession

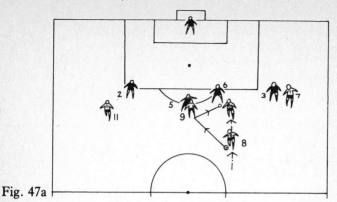

Fig. 47a

and tries to take a one-two off his centre forward colleague but, as explained, he dictates where the ball must be returned to, and running at the enemy defensive left half, the move easily breaks down.

If the attacking inside right has a good left-foot shot, then the coach can suggest that the space between the enemy defenders 2 and 5 might, in this situation, be productive. He can then take the players through the move described in Fig. 47b: the inside right plays to the centre forward who sprints to meet the ball and flicks it on first time with the outside of his right foot, playing it nicely into space for the inside right to shoot with his left foot, or go in closer if he can.

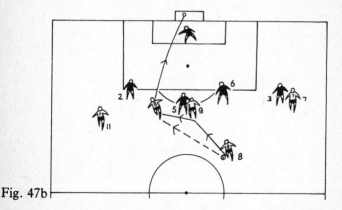

Fig. 47b

Better use of the space between the right back 2 and the centre back 5 can often be made, using the left winger or left centre forward. For the purpose of this practice, put it to the inside right that the left winger is relatively loosely marked because the right back has dropped a little to cover the centre, and suggest a cross-field pass to the winger. Now the enemy right back will get tight on the left winger and, judging the moment, before he gets too close, the left winger plays the ball off to the centre forward, who, as always, sprints to meet it. Screening it from his opponent with his body, he plays the ball off, first time with his left foot, into the space behind the right back, to put the winger in, as in Fig. 47c.

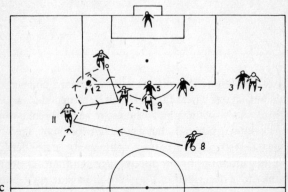

Fig. 47c

The customary Continental European defence, with a *libero* standing back, should in theory be better equipped to deal with one-twos for, whether the wingers are used, or (as in Fig. 48) the midfield men try to play one-twos off their centre forward, the free back is better placed to cover on either flank. But to gain this advantage, the free

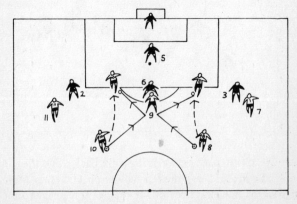

Fig. 48

defender must position himself further back than the typical British sweeper, in order to give himself time to go either way successfully. This gives the attacking side marginally more space to play in, and of course no defender or defence is infallible.

If such one-twos like this are practised by good players who understand what is involved and make sensible decisions about whom to play the 'one' to, and when to look for the 'two' back, then more good goals could be scored.

The very best Continental European teams have always been good at playing one-twos going into the enemy box. Playing for FC Bayern München at their peak, Franz Beckenbauer would often come forward with the ball at his feet, take a one-two off Gerd Müller and score a fine goal when his side needed one most. Regretfully, outstanding players like Cruyff (before he was twenty-six), Beckenbauer and Müller are becoming more and more difficult to find.

But there is no reason why good players, according to the level at which they play, should not have the skill and knowledge to pull off successful one-twos, provided they are intelligent and work with a good coach who believes in good, attacking football above all else, even at the very top.

Coaches who work hard with their defenders and leave the matter of scoring to the natural ability of their players are slowly killing the game. Ideally they would like to win every game by a 1–0 margin.

My experience of coaching one-twos at a high amateur level will probably echo that of other coaches who try it, for the players do it the way that suits them. The first thing I did was set up a basic defence with a goalkeeper, one centre back, and two full backs. I positioned myself as the free covering back, according to the natural skills of the players attacking, and instructed them to play a one-two off the centre forward or one of the wingers. The key to the natural attempt is determined by the player's best shooting foot. Thus, in the first practice, my right-sided midfield player came forward, gave a reasonable pass to the centre forward and, getting a good ball back in space, was able to shoot—because I had positioned myself between the right back and the stopper. Now I sent the same player back to try it again, but this time I moved across *before he started*, and I intercepted the return pass. The same thing happened with the players who favoured their left foot for shooting. Regardless of whether they were running to space or not, they played a ball and ran looking for it back—according to which foot they wanted to shoot with.

When all the strikers and all the midfield players had had this experience, once with me offering them their favourite space, and then the second time covering it, the players all began to get the idea, after I had explained that they *dictate* and must run at space.

At top level in every European country, the players are skilful enough and bright enough to respond to the ideas of the coach. There is no reason, unless the coach does not know it, why he should not coach this simple move. The best players would soon catch on. But regretfully, so many coaches do not know. And this applies equally to managers. They get their jobs at top level, based on their reputation as a player or with a paper qualification that is often not worth the paper it is printed on, and then, either through ignorance (mostly) or through choice, devote themselves entirely to tightening up at the back.

This is one of the biggest tragedies of the modern game.

But the key to good one-twos lies in the understanding that it is the runner who dictates where the ball must be played back to, and he *must* run at space.

IX · Giving a central combination an extra twist

Since Soccer Coaching the Modern Way *was written I have slightly adapted my approach to the central combination. This will be best illustrated by describing a combination that will almost certainly be new to anyone who did not see Peru play in the 1970 World Cup in Mexico.*

Having seen Peru's first game in Mexico, I was so impressed by the quality of their attack that I finished up watching three of the four games they played there. They were superb in attack, but let down a little by the back four, and very much so by some tragic goalkeeping errors. One move, discussed below, involving inside left Teofilo Cubillas and centre forward Perico Leon, was really first class. Time after time, with variations, they cut their way right through the centre of the enemy defence, doing it the hard way by attacking the centre (the enemy's strength) and playing it on the floor. Figs. 49a to 49f describe the variations used by Cubillas, 10, and Leon, 9.

Cubillas invariably started with the ball, for logically it is easier for an attacking midfield player to receive the ball at his feet than it is for a centre forward. Thus, in Fig. 49a Cubillas, 10, is running forward with the ball at his feet. In practising this combination a left-sided attacking player should be used, and at first there should be no

Fig. 49a

opposition at all. (This is an addition to what was said in *Soccer Coaching the Modern Way*: otherwise everything in that book about coaching combinations still holds good, but start each practice without any opposition at all.)

Left midfield player 10 runs with the ball at his feet straight towards the centre forward 9 (and, in matches, the stopper marking him). The centre forward comes off, moving to meet player 10, and then suddenly sprints across his path in a crossover, close enough to pick up the ball himself if necessary. This should be determined by whether or not player 10 (with the ball) is being hard-pressed by a challenging opponent. This point should be emphasized by the coach at the appropriate time and is easily understood by relatively intelligent players. But, for the purpose of this practice, player 9 simply runs across the path of player 10, feints to take the ball and, all in one movement, is gone, sprinting left. Player 10 then runs on a few yards more with the ball and lets fly at goal with a shot from around the edge of the penalty area.

As always when coaching combinations, the coach should give his sole attention to the players involved, in this case 10, 9 and the goalkeeper only. After three or four runs through this practice, when it is clear that both players understand what is required from them, the coach moves on to an alternative course of action. Now player 9 actually does take the ball off the toes of his colleague 10, still sprints away left with the ball while player 10 moves ahead, taking care to stay behind the ball and therefore on-side, as in Fig. 49b. Again, three or four runs at this should give the players the idea. The seeds have been sown.

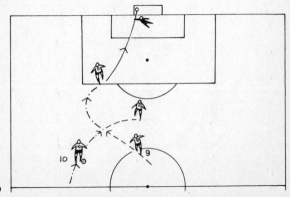

Fig. 49b

Now we return to the combination in Fig. 49a and go on to give it an extra touch as described in Fig. 49c. Here, after the paths of the two players have crossed, player 9 has only feinted to pick the ball off the toes of his colleague 10, and has sprinted away while player 10, still in possession, runs on 5 or 10 yards more and then gives a slightly reverse pass to player 9 who has taken care to be on-side. Player 9 now collects the ball, runs on, and shoots at goal.

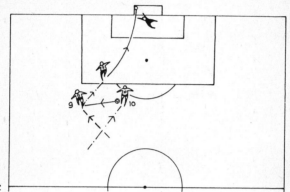

Fig. 49c

This variation may cause some difficulty amongst the players at first, but the coach should persevere, perhaps spreading his approach over two or more sessions with the same players if they show signs of losing interest because they cannot do it. Finally, he should switch to the alternative described in Fig. 49d. This starts again like Fig. 49a but for simplicity's sake we take it up at the point where the paths of

Fig. 49d

the two players cross. This time it is centre forward 9 who comes away with the ball, sprinting left with it under close control. Player 10 meanwhile runs on through the middle, taking care only to stay on-side in relation to the ball. After sprinting between 8 and 10 yards, player 9 gives his colleague 10 a reverse pass, and 10 collects the ball in his stride and runs on to shoot.

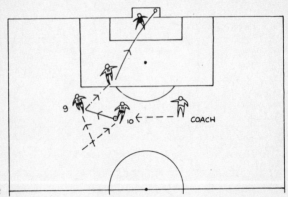

Fig. 49e

Once the players have reached the level where they can reproduce each combination as instructed by the coach, he himself should now provide minimal opposition. In Fig. 49e the coach has instructed the players that after the crossover it must be player 10 who carries on with the ball at his feet. Having positioned himself nicely before the practice began, the coach now moves across to offer player 10 a challenge and, judging the moment just right, not letting the coach get close enough to have even a nibble at the ball, player 10 gives the slightly reversed pass out to his colleague 9 who receives the ball in full stride and runs on to shoot.

After two or three runs at this, the coach should now instruct the players that player 9 must take the ball off the toes of player 10 (see Fig. 49f). Again positioning himself as indicated, the coach offers a challenge to player 9 and, at just the right moment, 9 passes to 10 who goes in to shoot.

Now we come to an improvement change from *Soccer Coaching the Modern Way*. Once the players have got the idea and can reproduce all the variations to order, the coach sets up a game four v four. One goalkeeper and one centre back (under orders to play only defensively) are allied to two attacking players. They play against four

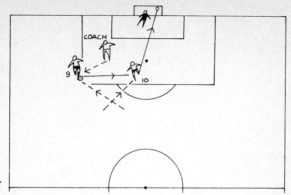

Fig. 49f

similar players, and the goalkeepers and defenders are instructed that every time they get the ball they *must* pass to the left midfield player (10 in the figures and practices).

The coach has to work doubly hard, unless his players are extremely capable, to get 9 and 10 to reproduce the combinations they have practised. This applies to all combinations, for this intermediate step helps the players in any combination they are coached at. He will almost certainly get a sore throat, for he must call to the players what to do before the ball comes and, almost simultaneously, must call to the player with the ball telling him what to do. Every call has to be in good time so that the player can respond, so this really is very hard work for the coach.

Now, by adding one defender and one more attacking player to each side, the practice can be extended to a five v five small-sided game. The central defender can also be 'freed' to play as he wishes. But, to drive home the work undertaken in the coaching session, this five v five game must be continued for players 9 and 10 only so that, whenever they get the ball, they must try to *reproduce their combination* in the new conditions. If, for example, the centre forward gets the ball he *must* always pass back to his colleague 10, and from there they will try the combination. Whenever player 10 receives the ball as a result of the natural flow of the game he should be under orders to work with centre forward 9 and try to produce the move in any of the ways that they have just practised together. Naturally it will have been sensible for the coach to have worked with two other players, say right winger 7 and midfield player 8, after each stint at working on the central combination with players 9 and 10. Now, in the five v five game, each pair of players can be instructed to try out what they have worked at, every time one of them gets the ball. The other players involved can also be instructed that every time one of them gets the ball he *must* pass to player 10 or player 8, according to which side he is on, and in this way the coach will see to it that the players he has worked with get plenty of the ball and ample opportunity to reproduce their combination.

To end the session, the coach can set up a full eleven v eleven game if he has the space and the players. But he can still talk the coached players 'through the combination' that he wants them to produce. It is hard work for the coach, but really worthwhile.

Now the scene switches to the next match. The coach should have a word with players 9 and 10 and instruct them to pull off their crossover whenever they get the opportunity. If it does not come in the first game, then the coach must keep at it in training until it does come.

When the coached players reach a point where they are pulling off this move five or six times in a game, then the coach can switch to coaching some other aspect of the game, perhaps with a new set of players. It is vitally important, however, that the coach has his eyes everywhere during match play, looking for the things he has worked at and wants the players to produce in games. What can happen, for example, is that after spending, say, twenty minutes per training session on the combination and alternatives just described, and then switching to something else in training, the players gradually forget this particular move and its variations. Typically, the coached players will produce the coached move perhaps eight or nine times in a game, once they have really accepted it and adopted it as part of their armoury. But in consecutive games it may be observed that they are slowly beginning to forget it until they reach the point where they try it only twice in one game, and only once (or not at all) in the next.

Looking for all the things he has worked at, the coach makes mental notes of everything while watching the games, and when the players begin to fail to reproduce the coached combinations, then it is back, say, to a four v four game, faced only by one centre back and under orders to produce this move every chance they get. With lesser players it may even be necessary to go back to the beginning and take them through the basic moves and alternatives without any opposition at all. But over a period the coached players will slowly change their habits and begin to play the way the coach wants them to. Indeed, after a lengthy period, say two or three years, the players will not know any other way to play. In my experience, the attitude of my players changed over two or three years until they could accept even defeat with good grace against a team of 'fighting footballers' who simply used the long ball and worked everyone like horses. They said within my hearing: 'Well they beat us, but they cannot play football.'

One of my players even gave up playing for the company team arranged by his employers for Wednesday afternoons. He ceased to enjoy playing with players who did not know what the game was about, and preferred to stay in the office and work, rather than 'play' with them, for he found that when he made runs, the ball didn't come. When he played a good ball, there was no one running into space for it. So he did not enjoy it at all.

When a coach has such experiences, as well as obtaining good results, then all the hard work is clearly seen to have been well worth while.

X · *Breaking through an off-side trap*

Playing against a very well-organized off-side trap can be more than a little frustrating. Apart from occasional mistakes which allow opponents through, however, two basic approaches to breaching an off-side trap can be coached.

In recent years the off-side trap has become a comparative rarity. Basically this is because the principles of having a free, covering player in defence, and playing the off-side game, are diametrically opposed. In the former the manager goes for cover, but with an off-side trap there is no cover at all beyond that which a goalkeeper can give.

As a player, I was myself a defender, playing at full back (mostly on the left), or at centre back. At full back, because I was able to look straight across the pitch, taking in everyone at a glance and able to anticipate what the opposition were going to do, I frequently used to call to a colleague in defence so that we moved up to catch an opponent off-side. At centre back I used to play a deeper game than most of my generation, and often found myself as the last man in defence. Indeed that is what I constantly tried to do—to be the last man in defence. This came about naturally, because although I was a little slow on the turn, I was very good at reading the game and therefore became highly skilled (and hated) at both covering and playing players off-side.

But as a coach and a manager I have always preferred cover to the off-side trap, largely because covering can be coached more easily, but also because the last man who gives the call to move up must be highly intelligent and able to assume an awful lot of responsibility. As a manager, I wanted the responsibility myself for what went on, and therefore I discouraged my players from trying to catch an opponent off-side—because the goal is wide open when it fails.

I liked the off-side trap as a player because it suited my abilities and my temperament, and also because in my formative years full backs were tubby little men with bald heads and bow legs—with football coming out of their ears, as we used to say. One particular player that I admired was the Scottish international full back George Cummings of Aston Villa, who had so much knowledge of the game in his head that it virtually *was* coming out of his ears. If only modern players could drop their pace and go more for thinking about the game!

In spite of the apparent contradiction between going for cover and adopting off-side tactics, there are a few teams that combine the two very well, perhaps because they have a back four who have played together for a long time and built up a good understanding.

I remember from my youth rare battles of wits between full backs like Cummings and inside forwards like Peter Doherty, Wilf Mannion and 'Raich' Carter. The full backs would vary their approach between providing cover and moving up, according to their reading of a situation. The great inside forwards would frequently receive a ball when in close support of their front three and, noting that the defenders were calling to each other and moving up, would feint to make a pass to a winger or the centre forward, before suddenly turning and sprinting with the ball at their feet straight at a gap in the line of defenders. From then on there was a rare panic amongst the defending side, everyone sprinting hard, trying to catch the player who had deceived them and was going through on his own—often to score a spectacular goal.

Nowadays the game is played so fast that only the really great players—and they are becoming rare indeed—have the ability to think at the necessary speed and take such decisions. But if a coach finds that he has an intelligent, highly skilled and quite quick attacking midfield player, he would do well to coach him in the art of going through alone at the appropriate moment. Even if the talented individual only makes his initial break-through near the halfway line and has not the pace to get in a shot before being challenged by a very quick defender, he might well be able to give a telling pass to one of his colleagues after breaking through the back four who have moved up hoping to catch the strikers off-side.

To coach the chosen attacking midfield player—and why not try it with them all?—simply set up a situation with a goalkeeper, centre back and a full back practising against a centre forward, a winger and the midfield man. The defenders should be instructed that as the midfield player 8 in Fig. 50a receives the ball from the coach (who should position himself nicely to be able to judge whether or not the players are off-side), player 8 looks up and shapes up to pass a long through ball for one of the strikers, moving towards goal, to run on to.

Being close to the defenders 5 and 3, and bearing in mind that both the last two players are running hard upfield to spring their trap, the attacking midfield player suddenly sprints through the gap between them, heading straight for goal. With luck, the player with the ball at his feet will break through completely, for the strikers cannot be off-side unless the ball is passed to them.

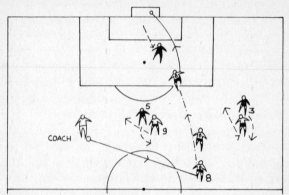

Fig. 50a

If the player with the ball at his feet is quite quick he will break through, leaving only the goalkeeper to beat—who must come off his line and advance to narrow the angle, and thus give the attacking player the chance to chip the ball over him.

The same basic idea should be practised on the left, using the left-sided attacking midfield player, the centre forward and left winger, against the goalkeeper, right back and centre back. If you play with full backs who are encouraged to attack, it will be worthwhile showing them the idea, too, for they may quite often find themselves around the halfway line in possession and be able to break through an off-side trap by feinting to pass and then sprinting away on their own.

When the player with the ball looks up, considering what to do, and decides to try and go through alone, it will be a good idea if, for example, he looks in the direction of the centre forward and calls his name, shouting 'Go, John' as if he were going to hit a long ball. This will often help to convince the defenders that he really is going to pass—before he turns and sprints away.

Finally, although I would not suggest that it be coached, I remember a highly intelligent and very amusing 'off-side' incident from the past. A Scottish international inside left used just the feint advocated to draw an off-side playing defence forward before going through alone. The defenders stood appealing in vain to the referee that the strikers were off-side, while the inside left ran on with time to spare in oceans of space. The opposing goalkeeper did everything just right, coming off his line at the right moment and, with the Scotsman some 10 yards from the penalty area and the goalkeeper just inside it, the man with the ball suddenly stopped and, putting his foot on top of the ball, flicked it up by rolling his foot over the ball and drawing it back; then, quickly getting his foot underneath the ball, up it came. Clearly the Scotsman was going to lob the ball over the goalkeeper's head, and realizing this the goalkeeper turned and sprinted back towards goal, his arms outstretched hoping to save the lob. But as soon as the goalkeeper had turned his back on him, the Scotsman gently pushed the ball forward and followed up the goalkeeper with the ball at his feet until the goalkeeper, reaching the goal-line, was totally bewildered. He turned round to see what was happening, turning his right shoulder first to find the Scotsman, and as he did so, the ball was rolled gently into the corner of the net on the other side.

This is one of the moments I shall treasure all my life for I have never seen it done before or since. And they played for League points in those days too, but at such a pace that their skill and intelligence were allowed to come through. Nowadays, if a player does not know what he is going to do before the ball comes to him, he is not allowed to play.

The second way that a player can be coached to break through an off-side trap is described in Fig.50b. Here again it is the attacking right midfield player who has the ball, received from the coach. It is a little more complicated and difficult to achieve than the first suggestion, but I have actually seen this tried with some success in recent years against packed defences.

Player 8 moves forward slowly with the ball, surveying the field in front of him, feints to pass, calling the name of the colleague he is pretending to pass to, and then suddenly plays a square ball for a player who was free and had already been picked out, in this case player 6. Player 8 should start this move well inside his own half for player 6 has to chip the ball high over the line of defenders first time—and the ball must have time to get to him before player 8 reaches the halfway line. Properly timed, player 6 produces his chipped pass at a moment when player 8 is still in his own half and therefore on-side, and sprinting on receives the ball in space, well beyond the line of defenders who have all been caught running the wrong way and must now waste time turning and getting off the mark if they are to catch him. I have seen goals scored with just this move,

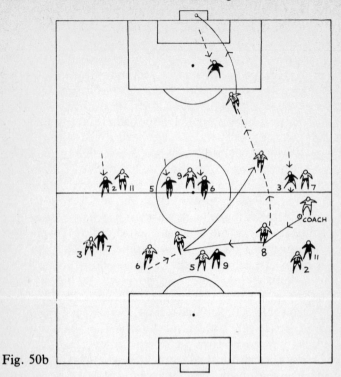

Fig. 50b

and on many more occasions I have seen the attacking team get very close.

One final point that will help a lot is that when the striking players 7, 9 and 11 see this square ball played in midfield against a team that has repeatedly caught them out with their off-side trap, all three strikers should sprint back with their markers and try to stay on-side. Above all, none of the strikers should make any move at all towards the ball because referees today are not as good as they were and might even blow for off-side despite the fact that it was player 8 who actually received the ball. If the strikers run away from the ball they are showing even the most inexperienced referee that they are making no attempt whatsoever to play the ball or interfere with the play.

As well as being very useful in midfield, the practice outlined in Fig 50b can be used very well when the attacking team have taken a corner or free kick that has been half-cleared to players 8 or 10, and the defenders are running out quickly trying to leave the opponents off-side. The man who receives the ball picks out a colleague square of him, plays the ball, and sprints away looking for it back, played well up over the heads of the defenders. To lessen the risk of off-side it should be played first time, with a nice chip.

Of course you require intelligent players for this, for breaking down an off-side trap is never easy. But if the players have been coached to cope with a defence that is known to play the off-side game repeatedly, having scored or gone close a few times, the opponents will almost certainly decide to abandon their off-side trap to the advantage of our team who can now get back to playing in their usual style.